Valérie B. d. Gasparin

Human Sadness

Valérie B. d. Gasparin

Human Sadness

ISBN/EAN: 9783337368906

Printed in Europe, USA, Canada, Australia, Japan

Cover: Foto ©Andreas Hilbeck / pixelio.de

More available books at **www.hansebooks.com**

HUMAN SADNESS.

BY

THE COUNTESS DE GASPARIN,

AUTHOR OF "THE NEAR AND THE HEAVENLY HORIZONS."

'Mi ritrovai per una selva oscura.'
DANTE.

NEW YORK:

ROBERT CARTER AND BROTHERS,

No. 530 BROADWAY.

1864.

CONTENTS.

INTRODUCTION.

APPINESS is as the glory of the sunshine, and when I picture to myself the happy, I seem to see one of those antique festal processions whose mazes come rolling on by the side of the shining sea, beating the air with thyrses, all garlanded with flowers. It is for these that the lustre of the day is made; their steps raise perfumed breezes, they move circled with harmonies, their faces beam, that supreme grace of joy and liberty floats upon their track; as they draw near, the intoxicated glance hastens onward to meet them, and when they have passed, it follows after them long.

But there is yet another phalanx, and this too I know well. This walks in the pallid twilight, keeps solitary paths, moves on, gloomy, silent, shuddering; it is much if some star sheds a spark

A

on its way, and even that ray alarms it; no song
accompanies it; if we listen, we only hear a sound
of dull and lagging footsteps, as of those that are
weary. He who should look closely would distinguish dejected brows; in those downcast eyes
—tired, one would say, of seeing—he might surprise some furtive tear; I know not what of faded
and of chill hovers over it; at its approach a void
is made, every one moves away in order not to
meet it. It is the band of sad souls, and at one
bound my whole heart has sprung towards it.

These last I recognise; they are of my kindred.
While joyous, and passing on in the triumphal
march of life, they had no need of me, I had no
need of them. A tear has fallen : Ye weep ! ye are
my flesh, ye are my blood ! my hands are stretched
out towards you; they tremble, they are weak,
weaker perhaps than your own; but take them,
will you not?

Sad ! How completely this one word is the very
secret of our day ! Flourishes of trumpets, cries
of the chase, bursts of orchestral music; gallop of
race-horses; shouts of laughter, racket of gaieties,
there is nothing else to be heard. The clamour is
at the highest, when lo ! a note rises, swells, pierces,
overpowers; ever more and more heart-rending;
an agonizing note, the cry of the distressed soul
lamenting in the midst of pleasures.

And yet it is not the most unhappy that are the most sad. There is something worse than the pangs of misfortune, there is the passive state of a subjugated heart.

You have given way beneath the burden of the days ; you have experienced this incapacity of re-sistance ; these latent sufferings, this pack, that does not bark but rends, has fallen upon you. Passers-by look at you, and remark : There goes one of the happy ! God sounds your spirit, and says : This is a sufferer !

It is to you that I come. Others, better author-ized, will dress more open wounds. Great griefs have their acknowledged place in open day, the care of them belongs to great Christians. The lesser draw near to the small; they listen to those complaints which men occupied with grave affairs have not the leisure to hear. The anguish that is dumb, the torments that are hidden ; all that is agitating itself, all that is struggling beneath life's calm surface,—this the lowly can understand, for this they have felt.

It does good to weep in company.

Do you remember that picture by Bendeman, *The Jews beneath the Willows of Babylon ?* The four figures are mortally sad ; and yet they give one a sensation of peace, of, as it were, the ideal light of heaven. This comes of their having met, of their eyes having recognised each other, of their having wept together.

Come, then, let us press very closely each to the other, and like them weep together.

Will you allow me an illustration? It alone can describe what I am; it alone can express what I desire.

The Desert stretches out implacably around; the day has that fierce character that arises from an earth and sky on fire; a caravan approaches, the sand that it disturbs rises, wraps it about, and falls back upon its track effacing it; the camels drag on heavily; the men sit bent in two, they say nothing, look at nothing; they let themselves be carried on, that is all. Meanwhile a figure that had kept in the shade beneath a great rock has risen; as the caravan passes, this figure stretches out its hand, and offers a vase full of water; the cup is poor indeed, but for all that the men steep their lips therein, and when the caravan has resumed its march their heads are lifted.

I.

OPPRESSION.

O not expect a rigorous classification. I am not good at numbering sorrows; and besides, you would not thank me for doing so.[1]

Amidst the sufferers of this world, I meet the flock of the oppressed, and I halt beside them.

These, of whom I am about to speak, are neither the oppressed crushed by a brutal tyranny, nor the oppressed terrified by the threats of a violent will.

[1] The author obeying, almost unconsciously, that law of sympathy which transports us into the heart and the situation of others, has constantly allowed the sentiments here expressed to assume a personal character.

And yet nothing can be further from an autobiography than this little book. If the soul from which it emanates feels itself profoundly human, burdened with the same vexations, wounded by the same blows, bowed down by the same weaknesses that attack other souls, it, nevertheless, neither lays claim to a monopoly of sufferings, nor to the weight of

There is a hidden oppression which weighs silently upon the soul, sometimes upon the life itself, and that our tribunals do not punish ; it is this that I complain of.

Have you ever sounded the depths of that word, *La Gehenne ?* The soul impeded, the heart straitened, every movement compressed, a stifling weight upon the chest—there you have it. The good old times, who understood it well, used to call one of their worst tortures by that name. At the time I write, this torture exists still, and you might find thoroughly respectable people, inhabiting fine houses, beautifully dressed, the smile on the lips, who for all that are suffering *La Gehenne.*

A spider's web weaves itself about your freedom ; invisible threads interlace each other ; you do not actually feel them, only you breathe with difficulty ; one morning you breathe no more. Or else it is some hindrance that impedes your activity. Your thought, that queen of the air, at every flight it

all the sadnesses, nor accepts the taint of all the wickednesses that afflict society.

One may know pain without having endured all its forms.

One may be a poor creature, often buffeted by the enemy, without having actually succumbed in every encounter.

One may point out horrible poisons without having imbibed all their venom.

There is therefore no confession whatsoever to be looked for in these pages ; they only contain a spontaneous burst of sympathy for those who suffer.

takes, falls back inert ; your nerves are paralysed ; and your soul, like a lion shut up in a cage, at first roars with indignation, and dashes itself against the bars, then, wearied out, exhausted, cheats its despair by that monotonous to and fro which helps us to stupefy our vital energies.

From wherever it be that oppression emanates ; whether it be exercised by persons or things ; whether it choke us by one of the thick atmospheres laden with narrow ideas, or take a definite shape and accent, enclosing us in the grasp of a rough hand ; whether it be the health of others that imposes it upon us, or some morbid affection of our own poor brain that subjects us to it,—you have surely felt it,—I have met with it,—no one escapes from it.

And, singular fact, it generally happens that this oppression that I allude to comes to us from below. It is the best natures that are the easiest enslaved; inapt to resist, harassed by scruples, astonished at audacities they have a difficulty in comprehending, their very delicacy prepares their bondage. Little qualified to defend themselves, they are well qualified to suffer ; the friction which would hardly be felt by a less exquisite epidermis lacerates them ; the weight that one of those muscular heroes, who laugh at our feeble limbs, would lift with a finger, leaves them prostrate on the earth.

It is difficult for power to avoid despotism. The possessors of rude health; the individualities cut out by a few strokes, solid for the very reason that they are all of a piece ; the complete characters whose fibres have never been strained by a doubt ; the minds that no questions disturb, and no aspirations put out of breath,—these, the strong, are also the tyrants.

For my part, I only know one absolute sovereignty that respects the liberty of the humble. It is that of the Almighty,—He oppresses no one.

I tremble before man, the most brutal scares me most ; I do not tremble before my God. I, worm of the earth,—I retain in his presence the fulness of my independence. The very silence .of man has often crushed back my thoughts, my God never stifled one. He is on high, I drag myself along in the dust, nevertheless beneath his glance my heart beats high ; I dare to speak, to reply ; I dare, I might almost say, to dispute with him ; he does not overwhelm me ; he contracts, as it were, in order to meet me ; he explains himself to me ; he would have me won, not conquered ; and where God, the Eternal, deigns to abase himself, even to asking from me the consent of a cordial obedience, man rears himself to his fullest height, knocks me down at one blow, throttles me, and if I struggled would kill me outright.

But I live on, and I live chained.

On you too they have weighed, those leaden skies that oppress our existence. Everything was made for enjoyment ; a heavy cloud approaches, darkness descends, it grows cold. What has happened ? Some one has interposed himself between me and my sun.

We seem to owe even a deeper grudge to those that prevent happiness than to those who destroy it by attacking it openly. Without them, all would go well. Life is full of smiles : I love, I am loved, I desire to serve my God ! Suddenly an opposition arises, a jealousy of my joys, a mistrust of my heart ; a supposition of evil, a censure, an unkindness ; my sun has disappeared. And this oppression is one I must needs respect, for its hand is upon me. I may not close my ears and hear it not ; I cannot pass on and see it not ; it holds its place at the hearth ; its voice is loud, authoritative. I have tried to content it with appearances, it insists upon realities ; I have glided over things immaterial, it leans its whole weight upon them. I have sacrificed one after the other, piece by piece, to save my true treasure, many objects of less value ; the enemy has taken them ; but it is ambitious, it marches on, approaches, soon its frozen sceptre will be placed upon my heart. And in this silent conflict. of which nothing is to ap-

pear, I feel not only my happiness but my soul
decline, my strength fail, my energy become extinguished ; torpor succeeds to resistance, all movement ceases, scarcely do I even breathe ; I assist,
passive, and, as it were, unconcerned, at the deterioration of my whole being.

Alas ! there exists more than one oppression.
There is the oppression of commonplace ideas,
which lay down their own level, and remorselessly
lop off whatever outgrows it. There is the oppression of coarse minds, who impose their own
coarse vigour upon the weak. There is the oppression of incomplete natures, who go on straight
before them, breaking and bruising without mercy,
because they lack ears to hear. There is the oppression of a haughty, prosaic spirit, that with a
mocking smile withers up all that it fails to comprehend.

This last form goes deeper than any of the rest.
It plunges into the very recesses of your heart ;
you have not spoken, but it has found you out ;
it drags your idols into broad daylight, and turns
them into ridicule ; it enters irreverently into that
realm of the ideal, where you only venture with
timid step, and scatters to all the winds what it is
pleased to call the mere tinsel of a booth at a fair.
Who has not experienced those invasions of hostile

natures : ' I heard a language that was not my own !' Alien voices, characters fundamentally different ; yet worthy people, that one must needs esteem. And thus life is ruthlessly broken into, the life of the soul ; for you will not be able to find yourself again, and that is the supreme misfortune.

That last asylum, my thought, is violated. The moral atmosphere, like the physical, becomes impregnated by certain aromas. When you love, the look, the voice, the ideas of the one who is dear to you, hover, one would say, around you ; even when he is absent they rule you still. And this is your happiness, and the air that you breathe is so completely permeated thus, that nothing belonging to you can escape the subtle action. Deleterious influences exert the same power.

People say to me, There you are alone, there you are free ! Alone, however, I am not. Sarcasms ring around me ; rude contradictions discourage me from thinking ; I know not what miasmas float hither and thither in the air ; they have poisoned me ; I do not recognise myself, I do not belong to myself any longer ; the absent rule over me; a train of ideas opposed to my own passes, seizes me, and drags me along ; they get a hold upon me by force of antipathy, just as others possess me by attraction. ~ And besides, my life does not belong to myself; my masters will soon be back.

Who has ever envied the brief leisure time of a slave ? the yoke has indeed fallen off for a moment. but the shoulders remain bowed, it is impossible to stand up erect.

All this is weakness, nothing more !

What ! am I then writing for the strong ?

But despotism is not always of so subtle a character. Here, for instance, is a pedantic, heavy opposition ; that attacks each word as it takes flight ; that rivets every idea to your lips ; thought can henceforth only issue armed for war. Farewell easy chit-chat; farewell unfinished sentences, and all that freedom of the mind, and that carelessness of language, and those chance sallies, and that self-forgetfulness without which there is neither gaiety nor grace, nor talk worth having. You discuss, then you dispute, then lassitude seizes you ; you keep yourself quiet, and in the silence that prevails, the heavy hammers of pedantry, beating the empty anvil, end by deafening you outright.

Or else it is thus no longer ; no one is giving you a thought, only an ill-conditioned temper is exercising itself, and scolding on its own account. The daylight blinds ; the breezes congeal ; the green of the field wearies ; the shades of evening sadden ; the flowers asphyxiate ; the birds sing too much; the dew wets; the road has stones; the path briars; no laughter enlivens; joy is an offence; this person is determined to quarrel with existence, to remain all bristles and disaffection, and, lo and behold! here am I no longer inclined to amuse myself, or to chat, or to be happy! An eclipse has taken place, and, as when the sun begins to go down we see the frightened birds fly here and there seeking a hiding-place among the branches, so all that stirred within me, all that came and went freely to the light, is scared, and then buries itself in the recesses of the heart.

Oh yes! I understand you; one should glide by, pass on, look elsewhere, and go on vigorously inhaling large draughts of the genial air that plays upon the earth! Yes truly; go tell the wild creature which the hunter is smoking to death in its hole to enjoy the fragrant breezes of the forest glade!

And moreover, do not press me too hard, or I shall class you amongst the race of oppressors. And indeed, may you not chance to be one of those intrepid champions, conquerors in every ring, for whom weakness is cowardice, all suffering whatever an imaginary evil; one of those who are exacting, because never having known failure; characters of bronze, rough to the feeble; one of those to whom the office of attendant upon the sick is supremely repugnant, and who when they see their neighbour on the ground, knock him up again by a blow !

I have known the oppression of evil ; by which I do not mean the tyranny of one's own vices, but the fatal influence of one of those personalities whose vicinity stirs the dregs of the heart. An infernal leaven ferments in such ; as soon as they draw near, you feel the mire within you begin to bubble up. The angels of God soothe us as they pass ; the very wind of their wings refreshes our souls : but there are angels of darkness as well ; these cross our sky, and the thunderbolt follows in their train.

People have wondered at family antipathies ; they have asked how those that everything— life-interests, occupations—tended to unite, should ever have come to hate each other. The galley-slaves also are closely bound together ; do they love each other any the better for that ? For my part, I have always been surprised at this passage of Scripture : 'If ye love not men whom ye have seen, how shall ye love God whom ye have not seen ?' Alas ! the more I know myself, the more I detest. As for the absent, I can without effort represent them to my mind as good, compassion-ate, generous, easy to live with. But this indivi dual who weighs me down, from whom not one portion of my life can escape, oh, how difficult

I find it to love him, seeing him as I do so
near !

To love ! In these great shipwrecks of our independence, methinks I have hit upon the word that
will save us ! But to love is just what I cannot do;
what often I do not even wish to do. And yet,
my God, if I hate, mine is the most abject and
utter bondage. As soon as I love, everything becomes possible to me. In vain would the one I
love seek to wound me ; I should not heed the
wound ; should he exact much, I have given him
more ; he refuses to understand me, well, I will
understand him ; he mistrusts me, I believe
in him ; he hopes for nothing, I, I hope everything.

This is Christian Charity that you are describing. I know it is ; and as far, indeed, from my
depressed and resisting heart, as the starry firma-
ment is far from the abyss ! But this is what I do;
on my knees, hands clasped, I say to my God :
Thou who lovest me, enable me to love !

Oppressed by men, tyrannized over by ideas, I
am no less so by the course of daily life.

The agency of inert things enslaves me. My
soul is subjected to the coarse grasp of facts;
reality treads my faculties beneath its heel ; and
often withers what I have of best.

Is there not somewhere in your neighbourhood
one of those miserable existences that recall the
In pace of the Middle Ages? Not a ray glides
between the bars; if some chance blade of grass
tries to show green, a rude hand pulls it up; nothing sings there; all tendernesses are crushed
back; duty bristles with watch-dog growls; one
dare not stir, and still less complain there; movement would be considered audacity; a murmur
would pass for revolt; nothing is to be done but
to walk on, head bent, along the sombre tunnel.
And all the time one had a heart, and there was
a sun in the sky, and one might have bestowed
happiness, and one was conscious of energies, and
one had to shut one's-self up, to grow down, to close
one's eyes, and the sap repressed turns to poison!

Or, if this be not the case, there are the exigencies of a high-pressure career which swoop
down to crush some peaceful nature, fond of
silence and solitude. It wanted the shade,—
modest occupations, some leisure; it asked no
more; under these conditions it would have blos-
somed out; its very progress depended upon its
obscurity. A whirlwind sweeps it away; it has to
be here and there; each day brings it some fresh
care; it may not breathe freely; it has not the
right to do so. Anxious, bewildered, too timid
to resist, believing that it beholds God's decree

wherever the feverish activity of the age is harshly laying down the law, it consumes itself, restless in its agitation, paralysed by excess of movement more than others would be by the immobility of death.

You have met some of these elect minds; intellects made for thought, creative imaginations. These were soaring on vast wings towards the higher regions, they seemed made for free space as the eagle for the luminous plains of the air; suddenly they are hurled to the earth. Antagonisms from below rise up against them; what not—some profession, perhaps, that one dislikes, yet which one must adopt; indigence that ties you down at once to the ground; the impoverished sphere in which one has to live; vexatious yet inevitable duties; and the soul writhes beneath the fangs of that pitiless force—necessity.

Alas! I see approach a heavy instrument of oppression, an enormous wagon laden with ingots. One hears the springs groan beneath the burden; wherever it passes, the soil sinks; if by chance a flower were growing there, it is crushed out of sight. Some look on at its progress more surprised than dazzled; others fix on its sides, all streaming with gold, looks of burning desire; nay, some there are that its aspect maddens outright,—these throw themselves beneath the wheels, and let themselves be crushed by the idol.

As a matter of fact money in itself will only be found to oppress fools. But in the hands of will, of passion, where it is personified in a character conscious of the sceptre it holds, money becomes a despot. Just because it possesses all the sources of material life ; grants or refuses enjoyments ; covers the sun beneath a cloud, or reveals it at will ; above all, because it realizes in a moment all the conceptions of fancy ; because it embodies ideas ; because the brute force of accomplished facts are under its jurisdiction ; it weighs upon general questions ; it solves problems as it pleases, sometimes giving out truth, sometimes error. Even those whom it seems to obey, money really leads in a leash ; the arts that it favours feel the pressure of its heavy hand ; something like a bag of dollars oppresses the mind that it emancipates.

Doubtless there are rich men who are truly liberal ; but these are terrified at the power money confers upon them, and by incredible efforts they shake it off. An empire based entirely upon indigence and weakness, or upon human degradation, makes them sick at heart. Distrustful of themselves, jealous to preserve intact the rights of conscience, the independence of thought, they

introduce an infinite scrupulousness and excessive
reserve into the influence they exercise. But such
as these are rare ; few men reach absolute power
with impunity ; and wherever the flood of riches
rolls and swells, on all the shores beaten by that
capricious tide we see drifted wrecks and meet
with bodies of the dead.

Existence knows other secrets wherewith to lay
us low.

The fatigues of the body help to aggravate the
dependence of the soul ; youth loses its leaves as
flowers do ; vigour to bear departs in proportion
as the burden to be borne grows heavier.

Some characters had the cheerfulness of fine
summer mornings, when everything laughs and
sings ; in them even tears had the lustre of a fresh
shower ; for them, at least, we think, the days will
pass on smoothly ; life will touch them with a
mother's hand ; they are our joy, they are our
music ; if we merely see them smile, a light
streams about us. Not So ! they will bend, even
they, grow old before the time, and mortally weary.
Look closely; their delicate limbs drag the chain ;
some care already devours them, one of those
persistent griefs which seize hold of us at the
beginning of the journey, walk with us, sit, rise,
lie down with us, and bury us at last.

I am now going to mention a very puerile cause of oppression ; wise men will smile at it with pity. It is—shall I dare to say it—the tyranny of the atmosphere, neither more nor less than the weather,—the grey weather, the cold weather, the bitterness of the climate, and the gloom of the sky.

Oh ! how I admire individualities inaccessible to such follies ! But some there are that they affect profoundly.

We are inhabitants of the earth. When the soil grows hard and frozen, our whole being shudders ; when the spiteful east wind attacks us, even our best feelings decline ; when monotonous rains soak the meadows and fill the air with unwholesome damps, we are conscious of inexpressible languors. When a gloomy day dawns, when a thick curtain of fog fills all space, when we can no longer distinguish, through this diluted darkness,—with here and there a livid glare, either the skeleton of trees the winter has stripped, or that old wall where the ivy still hangs green ; when there are no longer mountains to lift our spirits, nor the sky to speak to us of eternity ; it is a fact, to our shame we confess it, that we feel oppressed. The enmity of the elements saddens us ; the incessant obstacles raised by the severity of an ungenial climate depress our courage ; this conflict for bare existence, this struggle, beginning the first thing in the morning, just as we awake into life, disconcert us ; and we are ready to ask ourselves whether it is indeed worth while to continue them.

No doubt man, a thinking creature, ought to float above the terrestial atmosphere, and all great minds do so ; but for all that, man has a body as well ; a poor body lacking wings ; its lips inhale the air of low regions; it is through its organs that sight reaches him ; its surface now dilates beneath the soft breath of summer, now shrinks and shivers beneath the rude winter blasts. Tell me if you will that the philosopher, much more the Christian, may find himself happy in a prison ; that a dungeon into which Jesus descends can grow radiant ; but do not tell me that a dungeon is not a dungeon ; do not tell me that those walls streaming with damp are as pleasant as a meadow where a merry brook is flowing, where honeysuckles wave, where spring breezes blow.

As for me, so far from condemning as puerile the sympathy of our human nature with the physical world, I find it a sovereignly harmonious fact. It occasions me suffering I own ; but it also affords me enjoyment. At times it crushes me, but there are hours in which it restores me no less. I would control it ; I would on no account destroy.

Would it, indeed, be well to do so ? Should we

not lose in sensibility what we might gain in strength, and is there not a certain hardness in those natures that are so vastly independent of the weather? I, for my part, discern the eternal wisdom here. Those who would have us indifferent to the sunshine, are the very people who would have us indifferent to the emotions of life. I cannot go their length ; whatever God has given me I hold to be good. He has made me a body, I accept it with all its liabilities ; He has made me a heart, and never will I stifle it.

Believe me, if a new planet were to be discovered and that you were informed that it rolled on, mere mud, far from the glorious light ; that tempests ravaged it ; that damp exhalations surrounded it ; and that there were living creatures there, inhaling those miasmas, and that that desolate expanse rolled through the void without meeting a ray, without any warm breath ever reaching its accursed soil ; you would shudder with horror ; angels would weep over it ! Very well then ! have pity upon us, and leave us our weaknesses.

See, the fog is rent asunder ; the vast azure reappears ; the young leaves sprout ; the lake grows blue ; we know how to suffer and complain ; we know too how to be happy and to give thanks. My glances lose themselves in the sky ; I plunge therein in thought ; I exhilarate myself with its

glories ; they sink into my very soul ; I am joyous now, ready for work, ready for combat. You
are the superior being I grant, always equable in
a temperate zone; I am but a poor creature of impulse, soon cast down, soon raised up ; neither of
us is condemned to be useless in God's great plan.

Shall I speak of exile ; of the oppression of
strange places ; of the hostility of foreign habits ;
of that dispossession of self that arises from being
dispossessed of our country; of that breath of
the soul which grows faint from contact with an
alien air ?

We may be expatriated without passing the
frontiers. Every nature whose laws are violated
is an exiled nature. God has placed pines on the
mountains ; he has planted the olive in the burning soil of southern zones ; let the gardener come,
let him bring down the pine to the hot plains, let
him force the olive to climb the cold heights, and
we shall see these stunted and distorted trees, the
pride of the horticulturist, the disgust of common
sense, protest with all the eloquence of their
withered leaves against such an abuse of power.

I recall to mind a poor cactus buried in an old
pot, which was catching its death of cold on the
wooden gallery outside a little inn at Zermatt. You
have doubtless seen it, this high Alpine valley in

the neighbourhood of Monte Rosa ; which con-
trasts the severe verdure of its meadows with the
dark blue of a sky shut in by snowy peaks. The
breezes of Italy which come to die there have all
passed over ice ; to the south Mont Cervin with
his inviolable pyramid closes it in ; the very sun-
beams there assume I know not what of austere ;
the flowers of our gardens, even those that resist
our winters, would not venture to show themselves
so high up ; it was there that they had placed the
poor cactus ! Shrunk, straggling, sickly, it was
trying to stretch out its wrinkled limbs beneath
a limpidly clear atmosphere which did not warm
them ; you would have said that it trembled. At
each puff of keen air which braced us up, us
mountaineers by birth,—the cactus shivered ; a livid
tint already bordered its leaves ; it was spreading
to its heart ; it was on the point of death. And
I had seen these gorgeous plants bending their
broad spatulas of gilded green over the blue
waters of the Mediterranean. I have seen their
vigorous trunks and their scarlet blossoms, and
all the exuberance of life-sap warmed by the
fervours of a tropical sun ; I have seen them
lift their broad outlines upon the burning sands
of Syria, and stand out in their savage luxu-
riance against the dazzling azure of an African
sky.

To weep with those that weep, is that to murmur ? Would I aggravate the evil that we endure
by the infernal oppression of a rebellious will ?
My God, thou knowest that so soon as I recognise thy hand, I bless it, I desire to adore it.
But thou permittest us to groan; in that, thou
showest thyself God and not man.

The soul that denies its suffering is ill prepared to find thee ; nay, will it even seek for
thee ?

Thou hast listened to the complaints of Job, the
sorrows of Daniel rose up to thee ; the more freely
they were poured out, the more perfect the submission of their heart. Hear us too, Lord ; thou
shalt soothe us as a mother soothes her child ;
when corrected by thee we shall become obedient.
Where our martyrdom was, thou shalt substitute
victory.

My glance returns to rest upon myself once
more ; a slave everywhere else, in my own heart
at least I am free.

Do not be alarmed, I will not repeat any of the
commonplaces of the schools. All that has been
said about the tyranny of passion, and the despotism of a perverted will, I hold to have been said
once for all. I am not treating of our sins, I am
treating of our sorrows.

Do you know terror? Has a dark thought ever seized upon you in the calm hours of life; one of those thoughts that pass over us like a simoom? Have you shuddered beneath its influence, have your knees refused to support you, have you remained prostrate as though some phantom hand had touched you?

It is night, everything is silent; my little baby breathes low and even; I have sons who are young and bold; that cherished being whom I love a thousand times better than myself, I possess him still; we belong to Jesus; eternity belongs to us; I listen to his respiration, it falls gently on my ear. If it stopped! If suddenly I heard it no longer! If sickness came, if death took away! It will come, it will take. A day will dawn when that beloved one, pale, consumed by agony, breathless —there, beside me—will look for me with eyes that can distinguish me no more. And I,—I shall watch his every breath, I shall see my life escape with his; I,—I shall not be able to hold him back, neither my cries nor my supplications will hinder God from doing what he will! And I shall remain alone, and I shall have to walk weeping along life's desolate steppes. Then I seek for my Saviour, and I find him no longer. I sought to seize the secret of the future; the secret of the future crushes me.

Or else it is some formidable circumstance that God holds off, holds chained from me; it is some influence from which he has delivered me; it is something that I dread, and against which his protection secures me. Will it always secure me? He has indeed pity upon me to-day, but will he have pity upon me to-morrow? Will not my sins tire out his patience? I seem to see approach the cloud from which the thunderbolt will flash. It bursts. Yes, there it gathers; my happiness is destroyed, difficulties assail me. The Lord has put his bridle into my mouth, he leads me whither I would not!

Lost, wandering in ignorance and darkness, bent beneath the rod which I feel to be lifted, which will strike I know not when nor where, I move in utter despair, hither or thither, according as the madness of my thought leads me on. God is my God no longer. Fate, that blind mechanism that has neither heart nor soul, that demon of dread, fills the sky with its sullen ferocity. My strength gives way, my faculties, my nature; all is crushed, all is oppressed!

Fool that I am, it is I that am my own oppressor! the hallucinations of terror have subjugated me.

There is another bondage that debilitates the soul, that of a besetting desire, a besetting thought.

Be it scruple, covetousness, anxiety, what you will, a file is gnawing away at the brain, a weight is compressing it. You seek to deny its existence, it proves itself by torturing you; you oppose your reason, your good sense, it laughs at your limping logic; you wrestle with it, the struggle gives it added energy. Whether you resist or succumb, the very fact that you have to measure yourself against it insures its hold upon you.

But these are absurd griefs!

I am perfectly aware of it.

These are imaginary sufferings!

Not so, you are wrong there. True, my judgment condemns me; I look upon myself as unreasonable, cowardly, ungrateful; nay, if you like I will call myself by still harsher names. But I have fought, I have returned bleeding from the conflict. Scarred, deafened, what with the cries of my conscience, and the barking of that unchained pack, I am at my wits' end. Tell me that I must resist to the death; do not tell me that such sufferings are nothing, that they do not burn, do not consume, for my torn and shuddering flesh is charred.

Imaginary! People think they have effected a cure when they have let that drop of boiling oil fall upon your wounds.

Absurd! My own common sense had told me

so before you, and that is the very thing that aggravates my torment.

I am wrong, you say, to suffer! Go, take that comforting opinion to the mutilated man who suffers terrible pain in the leg that has been cut off long ago. Prove to him that he cannot possibly feel anything, since the seat of his suffering no longer exists. Do you know what he will do? He will look at you, will pass his trembling hand over his forehead, on which stands the sweat, then he will turn on the other side, and speak to you no more.

In your place I for one should not be tempted! I should have no besetting idea! I should be contented with what I had! I should serve God faithfully! I should roll on smoothly along a road without ruts! You!—I have no doubt you would. Most willingly do I proclaim you better than I; wiser, nay, the only wise; whatever you will, in short; but I meanwhile am dying; my heavily laden breast can no longer breathe; I am wrong, no doubt, to be dead; you are right to be alive; only for God's sake leave me; do not crush the worm that Jesus is about to warm into life by His breath.

Have I come to an end of our oppressions? Not yet; the heaviest of all has still to be mentioned. No one person is guilty of it, but all in

their turn inflict it. Yesterday you underwent it ;
I shall do so to-morrow. It is the oppression of
constraint !

If you have the right to be unhappy, do not
complain ; the worst of all torments has not
reached you. Would you like me to show you
the truly tortured of this world ? Look at those
who laugh while devoured with pain. We belong
to this number ; we know what heart constraint
means. Oh, to weep at our will ! what would we
not give for such a privilege ; but this were liberty,
and this we have not got. The first indifferent
person that comes is master over us; he may break
into our life at any and every hour ; we owe him
a calm expression of face, pleasant words, and if
we fail to render these he will ravish our secret
from us.

Who is there that has not experienced the
implacable oppression of constraint ? Those internal desolations bursting forth beneath the
appearance of happiness, like a hurricane in
the immensity of some subterranean sphere, have
been suddenly unchained. For one moment we
were free to suffer, that interval of grace is over ;
we must re-enter common life, must have dry eyes,
the lips may not quiver; the ear must listen attentively ; the mind must take part in the puerilities
of conversation. And all the time a sob is there

ready to choke the voice; the tears are about to
overflow; and throughout the noise of words one
hears only one sound, one accent always the same,
that penetrates the heart.

Take care! the moment you are different from
the rest of the world, everybody is surprised,
and the surprise of other people is curiosity, and
curiosity is capable of cruelly audacious dealing.

History grows indignant over the exactions of
the ancient Romans. In those days the refined
classes that adorned the tiers of the circus, were
not satisfied merely to see men killed, their dilet-
tantism required something further.

Out upon convulsions, out upon the death-
rattle! it is only the ill-taught and ill-mannered
who abandon themselves to such commonplaces!
they, for their part, insisted upon the victim falling
gracefully, they had a right to that; woe betide
him who knew not how to expire according to
rule; hoots of contempt pursued him to the desolate shores of Tartarus. And we too, we have a
pitiless multitude contemplating us; the more
refined it is, the less it tolerates any weaknesses;
it permits us, indeed, to die, nay, sometimes it
demands that we should, but on no account allow
a sign of terror or a cry of anguish to escape you,
for that its nerves could not support.

Alas! this selfish and tyrannical crowd is general

indifference ; it is you and I ; we have these despotic appetites, and we have these susceptibilities.

One pities the frightful condition of the comic
actor, obliged to appear on the stage the day after
he had followed to the grave the remains of the
wife he adored. It would be difficult to conjure
up more agonizing circumstances. But has the
world who shudders at them ever thought of pre-
venting them ? And yet even under this borrowed
guise the actor belongs to himself. He has put
on a mask, beneath it his real face still exists ; he
has thrown himself into a foreign individuality,
which in some sense forms a shelter to the integ-
rity of his own character; he may indeed wear
festive attire, but his mourning is beneath it ; he
may smile, divert, act, his soul is still his own ;
his inner life is undisturbed ; no indiscreet question will lift the veil, no coarse hand will burst
open the gates of the sanctuary.

As for us, the comedians of this world, we have
not even this last inviolable retreat. The part we
have to play is not a mere recitation, it is a life ;
and, to say nothing of the careless and the indiscreet, many forcibly break into it whose invasion
is legitimate. How can we maintain the right of
reserve with regard to those who have the right of
search ? Shall I dare to say it, there is no more terrible inquisition than that of affection. For, after

all, we do belong to it; its treasure is our heart, and to deprive it of that is to defraud it of its due. Those who love us insist upon reading us. Indifference may be diverted, love cannot; love demands the reason of a sigh, of a pale cheek, and at the same time that it makes our happiness obligatory, it insists upon full confession as equally a duty. Love, like the sun, absorbs all clouds; to suffer in its presence is almost to do it wrong; at least it is to own that it is powerless to fill the heart, unskilled to heal it. There is occasionally a reproach, there is almost always some conceal-ment in the sadness of a beloved being.

You exclaim against these over-refinements! Well then, I will ask you if your sufferings do not mar the happiness of those who love you; if they can with an easy mind contemplate your sorrows; if, in unfolding to them a spirit full of gloom or grief, you would not utterly destroy their peace? No need of over-refinement to shrink from such consequences; they might well make the boldest hesitate. I am not here saying whether such con-straint is legitimate or desirable; I only say that it *is*. You yourself have experienced it; and, lips pressed close, hands clenched upon your breast, you have stifled your sufferings.

Oh be sure more than one among us sighs for the night, as the watchman of Judea did for the morning. We long for the shadows that may conceal tears; we invoke the darkness, which will give us back to ourselves; we yearn for isolation, to escape from slavery.

If this were all, ought we to be contented thus? Never! We need deliverance, we demand liberty.

Our generation has no fresh air, no breezes blowing; it is stifling, and it submits. Do not mistake its calm for the self-contained energy of those who control because they possess themselves; our generation is growing used to it; now to do this is to allow the irons to be riveted. Let us look our miseries full in the face. The thing to be done here is neither to yield supinely nor to rebel against God; nor to deny the fact of our suffering; nor to escape, by ceasing to be human, from the tyranny of people and of things. I prefer a man in chains, palpitating, and with heart full of life, to that nameless thing of abstraction, dryness, and selfishness, that the wise of this world are so diligently framing. We are impatient of chains, it is true; but better a chain, were it to leave its mark in blood, than liberty procured by the annihilation of the individual. Indifference is not independence. I insist upon keeping my predilections, and I will have my just antipathies; were they to torture me, I will hold them fast. Do not tell me of those solemn shadows that traverse society, proudly wrapped in their philosophical mantles ; there is nothing beneath them ; the drapery may indeed take majestic folds, but when the wind blows into it, you see a skeleton. The liberty we want is not that of feeling, still less loving no longer ; rather is it the faculty of feeling more and loving better. We are not anxious to escape from bondage by death ; no, but to trample it under foot, and swallow it up in victory.

Evils are evils ; despotism is unjust ; servitude is suffering. So much is certain. For me, I go to seek my liberty where it may be found ; I ask it from Him who has brought deliverance ; Jesus will bestow it upon me. He opens out heaven above my bent-down head. In vain may others hem me in ; no authority can prevent my soul taking flight, soaring, being mistress and queen in the region of faith, of thought, of love, and of true independence.

My soul having received the baptism of liberty, returns omnipotent. I have bowed beneath the yoke, a fiery circle shut me in, blank walls rose at the end of all my paths ; but when, in my despair, I lifted my eyes on high, when I cried to my God, a breath of life passed over me ; unknown horizons opened out, strength was given. I saw that I was not alone ; a tenderness, fraught with pity, warmed my heart. Before, I hated, now I begin to love. Those who oppress me have a soul, even they, an undying soul; I have prayed for them, and the moment I prayed for them, they ceased to torment me.

Nor shall things, any more than people, deprive me henceforth of my freedom. A blaze of light strikes on them, its brilliance reveals to me their true value; if they have rights over me I will submit; slavery consists still more in undue resistance than in servile obedience; if they usurp sovereign power I will shake off their hold.

Have I said *I?* What a misuse of language! I, I am impotent; I yield and I assert myself alike out of season; a straw can throw me down, an insect get the better of my life; but I have met the hand of my God; I belong to Jesus; I speak to him, he hears me; he wills my independence; he is well able to make me free.

Our age, which is inert, is also subtle. We have the effeminacy of the Lower Empire; we have its refinements too. We lack simplicity; we take neither people nor things as they come; the plot interests us more than the event. Feeble in action, strong in analysis, we dissect everything, and ourselves first of all. Energy is worn out by this process, and life escapes beneath the scalpel.

The solar microscope has been invented by science, but it is not science alone that makes use of it, everybody has one of his own that he applies to the infinitely little. There where the eye, as God has made it, sees only a grain of dust, a monster makes his appearance. Empty space is peopled with formidable creatures, on all sides, —claws, forceps, triple rows of grinders. These gigantic animals open monstrous jaws, their bodies wriggle, their tail, armed with a dart, is threateningly curved; the thousand facets of their eyeballs are fixed upon us; countless feet keep stirring, hairs bristling; and all this array of weapons is turned against us, and we stand terrified, gazing at the drop of water that contains such horrors. And all the time, that drop remains clear and undisturbed, and when our glances quit that atomic universe, to wander on familiar objects around, a smile replaces our alarm.

The moral world too has its atoms, imperceptible atoms that the over-excited vision of the soul changes into things of colossal size. Some hostility, for instance, was inoffensive while it passed unperceived; as soon as it takes shape, it wounds and prevails over us. That particular action left me unmoved, it was only a fact; as soon as I see an intention in it, my heart is irritated, my will assumes an attitude of defiance. Our visual acuteness, by exaggerating, doubles our sufferings. The primal harmony is destroyed ; there is no longer any proportion between our adversaries and our strength ; before the battle has begun it is lost by our own folly.

Slaves not unfrequently of a tyrant who does not exist ; dejected, overcome ; in piteous plight we fill with our complaints the free air in which we might stand erect.

Just as I am concluding, my thoughts revert, I hardly know why, to that old negro who is the very type of evangelical liberty.

He is beaten, imprisoned, sold ; his heart is full of sorrows, his body furrowed with scars ; half dead beneath the lash, sent hither and thither, passing from the hands of indolent kindness into the talons of ferocious cruelty ; each morning he loads his aged shoulders with his daily cross, he does not go to seek out other burdens. He accepts suffering ; he does not believe in evil. He feels, indeed, that he is ill-treated ; he does not poison his wound by applying to it the venom of distrust. Such as we see him, simple to innocence, good-natured one would almost say to inertness, he is his own master, his own king ; the harness of the slave in no way interferes with this ; the lash of his tormentor is powerless to prevent it ; insults glide over his tranquil spirit, the efforts of despotism are thwarted and vain. Uncle Tom towers supreme above the scenes of this world, and his fine old face will be always radiant with a divine splendour.

Only one word more; as it has occurred to me, I will even utter it.

We the oppressed—you, me—may we not perhaps be also in our turn some one's oppressor?

II

MISTAKES.

UMAN souls enter this life in pairs; arrived on the threshold of the world they take different ways; sometimes they meet each other again, these are the privileged; but more often they wander on at random: each beat of their wings separates them more widely; they traverse space disappointed and solitary, then disappear altogether,—this is the general fate! Thus speak the poets. I know a case more grievous still; it is that of a man who has run up against the whole world, and never succeeded in finding his true self.

Youth resembles a cross road; paths open out to the right and the left; which is the one to choose? Take a step to that side, and you are cried at, No! not here! Take the other side, still the same cry, No! not there! Perplexed, bewildered, you rush out the first way you can; the road leads to a quagmire, so much the worse, there you are, get out of it again or remain in it, that is your own affair.

To recognise one's-self and what one is fit for, that were, indeed, well; but in order to recognise myself I must have known, and as yet I have no self-knowledge at all.

Be like this one! be like that other! be like neither! that is what every one keeps repeating; very few say to me, Be what you are. Opinions generally received encumber my mind; whether I admit them or reject, my individuality cannot shake itself free from them. Desirous to please I have ears awake to praise; dreading blame, disapprobation discourages me; blind too, I burn to see; full of inexperience, I am full of good-will; my whole heart impels me to what is beautiful, what is admirable, but I am ignorant, I am timid; I have to confront adverse winds, the hail stings me with its sharp shafts; I hear sarcasms, and a fear seizes upon me; a certain shame of betraying my own feelings; a sense of confusion at being different from other people, and either I shut myself up or disguise myself, and in either case I am lost.

Have you never experienced it, that dread of letting yourself be seen as you are! The ardour of my soul, its generosity, the tender emotions that stir within my breast,—these are the very things that get laughed at! I will conceal them, I will bury them so well beneath an external disguise, that no glance shall find me out, no irony shall come and make my blood run cold.

No, truly, no one will find thee out any more, poor, bewildered heart; till thy latest hour thou shalt beat on beneath a borrowed mask. Oh how thou wouldst bless the holy boldness that should tear it off thee! How fain wouldst thou thyself dare to raise a resolute hand towards it, but no! what thou hast once determined to be, thou must be henceforth. What is it to others that you have made this fatal mistake? Such as you gave yourself out, as such they have taken you; the thing is done; you have the semblance you chose to wear; you have the character you have shaped for yourself; you determined to adopt a personality that was not your own; manage it as well as you can; it chokes you, stifles you; live, die, it is entirely your own affair.

It is only the strong who from the first can look themselves full in the face; they alone take possession of themselves, and this they do boldly: Here I am! I please you? so much the better; I displease you? so much the worse.

The weak, we who have all the tremors of
timidity, all the irresolutions of a morbid delicacy;
who are drawn in different directions, running
after our individuality, on this side and on that;
we resemble those legendary souls that went looking for their bodies. Here, indeed, it is the body
that is seeking after its soul; it is the uneasy
creature that calls for its spirit, and when by
chance the spirit answers,—oh misery! the former
. flies from it with terror, or repulses it with contempt.

You can remember, can you not, to have occasionally come into contact with those artificial,
distended faces, always the same, because the
blood did not circulate freely beneath the skin.

Can you recall any of those jesters by profession?
For the very reason that they were naturally sad,
easily moved, and that an arid breath chanced to
dry up their first tear, they have thrown themselves into an exaggerated gaiety. Their eyes
beam, their lips keep constantly dealing forth the
witticism or the joke; the lines of their face express an exuberant mirth, as soon as one sees
them, one's mood becomes light, one's talk jocose.
As to speaking to them of the sorrows of life, of
the anxieties of the heart, of what one hopes, of
what renders truly happy, who would think of such
a thing? Have they got a soul at all? there is
the doubt. We use language that they are capable

of comprehending—laughter, nothing but laughter. If one listened attentively, beneath those noisy bursts one might catch the wail of despair, but one does not listen. He anxious, he sensitive! He sad at heart! what nonsense! He is a thorough philosopher who takes life by the right handle; he is a social creature haunted by no sad thoughts, no poetical dream; he will never die of love, I'll answer for that; still less of melancholy.

No; only one fine morning he will blow out his brains. Then you will exclaim in stupid astonishment: Inconceivable! a man who was so gay! Exactly so, his gaiety and yours have killed him!

Or perhaps he lives, drags his clown's paraphernalia to the last. Follow him, however, into his own home. He has been diverting you all; your lungs are crowing still; you talk over the good stories he has told; the brilliancy of his witticisms still sparkles round you, his features moulded on a comic type expand again before your mind's eye; you laugh. Meanwhile he, alone at last, lets himself fall heavily into a chair. Why, what can he be doing? He is weeping bitterly. Oh! let him weep! He is free now, he is a man, he is himself. His face lengthens and sinks; you would not know him again, but how well he knows himself! With what frantic eagerness he returns to his own character! he is unhappy, he is passionately unhappy. More athirst for sorrow than others for joy, he plunges into that immense sadness, he finds in it once more his human dignity. And yet to-morrow! to-morrow, unless he has thrown himself into the arms of Jesus, unless he has asked him for courage to forsake those false colours he has been wearing so long; to-morrow he will again become what he was yesterday, the condemned to laughter, and he will laugh on till his heart breaks outright!

Or else take a different case. Another mistake leads me astray.

My soul is in love with the ideal; but what of that, the ideal is confessedly ridiculous. People positively tell me so, and I in part believe them. I am resolved to preserve this treasure of all chosen souls, but I will on no account have it discovered; I will not even have it suspected; and, accordingly, I make myself prosaic. Let us close doors and windows; let no air enter, for with the air the light would stream in, and if my idol were to be found out, what shouts of laughter it would provoke!

Or perhaps I feel a necessity of loving. To live alone with one other; to think with the same impulse; to have one heart between us; this is my day-dream. Fortune, success in life, I would gladly give them all for a humble little existence, hidden beneath the leaves. This is the very atmosphere that suits me ; so placed, I shall contend against evil and effect great things. Would you, indeed ? only wait a little. This is a mere idyl, this notion of yours; one reads Virgil, indeed, as a lesson in rhetoric ; but once a grown man, one leaves flocks to graze, shepherds to sing, and one becomes an official, a legislator, a senator if one can ; one gives parties, and marries a fortune, or if one does nothing of the kind, clearly one is an imbecile.

Come then, my heart, bleed inwardly; pass by, O ye bright luminous visions ! Perhaps, indeed, I shall continue to be an idiot as you call it. God grant me grace to do so, but you shall never know it. I will be the puppet that you would have me be ; my happiness, if it comes across me, will misapprehend me as all the rest do ; it will not find me out. It is only one more mistake ! Only one happy creature less ! What cares the world for that ?

Here again comes the stiffness of conventionality to paralyse a character all made up of light and motion. Spontaneous, unpremeditated, it has the gaiety of a child ; it has sadnesses as well, sudden bursts, impulses, enthusiasms, all of which

I grant you are not in very perfect proportion ;—
the laughter is sometimes a little loud ; tears come
like those thunder-showers that all at once drown
the sun out of sight ; but such as it is, it is natural
and it is charming. I add that when tempered it
is excellent, because it is true. Now then let
come traditions, let come the world with its good-
society amazement, and this poor soul perfectly
dùmbfoundered is afraid of being itself. Ere long
it grows ashamed of it ; it dares no longer laugh or
weep; it takes refuge in an artificial coldness. Here
and there some eccentricity,—one of those shoots
of impetuous vegetation which pierce through old
walls to open out to the light,—escapes in look or
tone ; instantly there is a hue and cry. Quick,
down with the portcullis, up with the drawbridge !
There where a coppice full of songs grew green, a
grey fortress is rising now ; passers-by measure its
height ; they feel an icy shadow fall athwart them ;
they quicken their steps towards the flowery fields
beyond. And yet a heart was beating there ; a
genial spirit gave out fitful rays ; there was life
still, there might have been happiness.

If, at the least, the mistake once committed might
become at length a kind of reality; if one but moved
freely beneath the borrowed garment ! But no ! it
was made to fit some one else ; we are not only
uncomfortable in it, but we are awkward as well.

These disguises only half deceive; they suffice to
embarrass; not to give one a home feeling of ease.
A false ring betrays an internal disorder. Not
being allowed to seem what I really am, I do not
even gain the poor privilege of appearing as I
should like to be. Something factitious exhales
from my personality, which achieves my deterioration.

Alas! and one may go on thus to the very end!
When the end is come, the indifferent crowd permits you to be buried without your disguise. Sometimes it happens that a curious on-looker stops
and contemplates you; sometimes at the supreme
parting hour a fold of the veil gets deranged, and
then your true visage appears. There it is, all
radiant, or all pale. There is the sweet smile;
when just about to be for ever extinguished, it at
length ventures forth upon the dying lips; the
glance is fraught with emotion, tears warm the
marble face! That then was the real man, the
real woman! What! so beautiful, so touching,
and I had never found it out!

Then the tomb closes, one goes away and one
forgets.

And just as there are souls who misunderstand
themselves, so there are lives that are one continual
mistake.

Such a one, for instance, throws himself into an existence that contradicts all legitimate desires, is fatal to all good instincts. He believes himself to be on the royal road, presses on; and when he finds out his error, he is too far from the straight way to return to it. And, moreover, a second nature has supplanted the first; the man groans and continues.

I have seen some of these misled travellers; and I shall never forget the bitterness of their smile, nor their melancholy glances that stray towards other horizons. For one moment they stop; you lift your voice appealingly : Come with us ! They shake their head ; they sadly give you to understand by a sign that they have heard you; ay, and it was just where we were going that they would fain have gone ; it was there that happiness awaited them. But no ! it is no longer worth the while ; they may just as well die of what has made them suffer so much and so long. Adieu ! And our eye follows their plaintive shadows sorrowfully and in vain !

This career entails atrophy of the heart ; these fictitious duties prevent me from fulfilling the real; each day beholds me of less value. I had once a soul, I do not know what has become of it ; money is crushing me; I am running frantically after some situation which will be the death of me ; I am lowering myself to obtain favours that I despise; subjecting myself to a brutifying employment; I possess myself no more. Were I to meet the man I am become, I should start back with horror; I take note of my own deterioration, like those old people, who, without power to arrest it, watch the gradual decline of their vital energies. Soon it will be over. I can at this very moment calculate the day when of all that was once me there will only remain a species of automaton, who will jot down columns of figures, or draw out reports, or compile materials ready to hand, or go on bowing and bowing, quite independently of any effort of mine! And I might have been a man!

Be so, for the love of God!

I! What would be the use of it? Once fairly merged in these deep places, there is no longer any heaven for me; all restorative breezes pass too high over my head; I bury myself up to the neck in the mire; perhaps I shall at last find myself comfortable there.

Alas! the joy of existence may be forfeited by many and many a different mistake.

Who does not pity the man of the fields when walled up in a town? His loved sun, the very same whose rays lit up woods and meadows, is quenched in fog. Instead of the fresh air, he has to breathe a fetid atmosphere; his eyes seek in vain for some vestige of nature, were it only a tuft of primroses, only an old tree trunk thrown down by accident; instead, they have to recoil from heaps of houses; they only meet rows of trees cut, drugged, clipped, tortured in every way. Oh how gladly would he give all those bright displays of flowers, methodically grouped, for the puniest sprig of blue sage, gathered in the first ploughed field that lies beneath a mountain breeze!

Look you, at this very hour the day is dull, snow covers the ground, the lake breaks on the shore with a monotonous ripple, sleepy tints cast their pale greenish lines across the water. It is all austere and sombre, and if you could see it, you would hardly repress a shiver. True, but there are boats plying against the severe background. Opposite me the immense Alpine range heave and pile up their immaculate masses. I inhale in free draughts an air that no one has ever breathed before me. My glance wanders over the expanse unchecked. There are forests down there; beneath those forests there are carpets of moss which no town feet have ever trampled. It is the free far country. The birds sing whenever they like, the honeysuckle twines its autumnal shoots where it will. The clematis is free to hook its trailing stem, with cotton-balls still clinging to it, as best it may. The oak stretches out broadly its giant branches, rustling with dead leaves. I am happy; God has made me for this. My heart breaks forth into thanksgivirfg. All at once that wretched life imprisoned in cities occurs to me. I see that man; he is transplanted in the dust of puerile, withering obligations; he is cheating his instincts by an unhealthy activity; not being able to procure solitude, he plunges into the very thick of the throng. All unrecognised wants turn to fever; he will come and go, and agitate himself continually. The poor fish, too, leaps and wriggles on the sand, but does it die any the less?

Ah! when it is God that decrees martyrdom, he blends his own peace therewith! But when it is man who mistakes and tortures himself, his suffering rages like a conflagration. No refreshing breath assuages the fierceness of the flames. To submit where God ordains, is the very height of energy; to accustom one's-self to the misarrangement of circumstances is the climax of weakness.

Shall I show you another unravelled existence? another of these unfortunates dragged along through a medium that kills him? Come then beneath this chandelier into this brilliant crush. Gold and jewels are blazing; costly vestments display-

ing their changeful sheen. You hear the orchestra
tuning; pleasure beams from all eyes; luxury gives
the stimulus to art; festivals have their poetry;
the day is too short; we escape from our very
selves. How, then, should we not lose all trace
of *ennui?* Visits, drives, twenty *salons* open at
once! I assure you that the hours are winged.

The hours are leaden. All this—I know it all
by heart. Everywhere the same figures, the same
tones, and this monotony kills me. If by chance
some face, some form, from some other circle,
should for a moment emerge into this blinding gas-
light, curiosity roused for a moment, soon satisfied,
relapses into torpidity and indescribable satiety.
There is nothing new beneath the sun! I turn
in my wheel—poor captive squirrel—convict
obliged to march on in the treadmill—what not?
I go on, always on. I had hoped to come to an
end, but there is no end to come to. Others
weary me, and I weary them. We are all playing
a comedy; nay, less than that, an insipid proverb,
the platitude of which turns us sick, and which we
repeat over again every evening. Do not speak
to me of the morning; it frightens me. And yet
no; if it did frighten me, it would at least give me
a sensation, but it does nothing of the kind. It
is the beginning of something that does not begin,
does not end, which harasses me, that is all. You

want me to read ; I have neither the wish nor the
power. You bid me walk. Does any one walk ?
You say, occupy yourself with somebody. Is there
anybody? Men are only pawns on the chessboard ;
women, dolls who roll their eyes. You would have
me to do something? Things have no longer
an existence for me. Formerly some of them
attracted me, and others repelled ; but at the point
that I have now reached, I defy any events whatever,—success, pleasure, catastrophe, whatever it
be—to make any impression upon me. You talk
of ideas, but to have an idea you must have first
of all an intellect ; of sentiments, but to feel them
there must needs be a heart. Of interests ! What
would you have me interested about ? About other
puppets disporting themselves on some other
stages ? You insist that God had not created me
for this. That may be. That I was once better !
Perhaps so. One thing is certain, that I am now
good for nothing, and care for nothing. Take my
word for it. You may show me the abyss if you
will. You will get nothing by it ; I see it, and
yawn. You point me out heaven ; I contemplate
it, and go on yawning.

Stop ! I know your disease, and it is a horrible
one. The enemy has deceived you, you have
mistaken your life ; you thought you were steering
toward the light, and you have lost yourself in

darkness. You are dying in the hell you have made for yourself, and you are afraid of leaving it. I tell you I know you well, and I experience for you a boundless pity. You no longer feel anything, did you say? You were lying to yourself. You are unhappy, fearfully unhappy. You stretch out your hands towards your wasted youth; you would buy the power to transform it with your heart's best blood. The future appals you, in your hours of solitude; broken fragments of prayer escape from your lips. No! your heart has not ceased to beat; when angels of goodness, nobleness, poetry, traverse the sky, and a reflection from their beauty lights up your brow, you lift that brow, and you follow them with a lingering look. You resemble those lost souls of the poet that run along the shore. The boatman passes, passes with his bark filled with valiant men, and because he has not seen you, because your first cry was lost in the noise of the oars, you become hopeless of yourselves; you repeat, in broken accents, that it is now too late; and, sunk in weakness and dejection, you weep. Nay, deny it not, I have seen you weep.

Courage! the boatman will take you in. Rise, for the hour is come. It is always the right hour to become men once more. Walk upon the waters; if you sink, believe me, Jesus is there. Breast the waves boldly, the bark is waiting for you.

He has reached it! eager arms have been stretched out; they have clasped him; a genial warmth revives him; youth returns. Strong men, ye, the workers of the world, receive him into your ranks! A shout of victory echoes round; I have found my way! There is a God! There is such a thing as happiness!

But all mistakes whatsoever do not originate in ourselves. The world is mistaken in its turn. Serious misapprehensions brood over men and over things.

As to ideas, this in no way disconcerts them; you may calumniate an idea, but if it be a true one it will recover itself; time has nothing to do with the matter, for ideas are immortal.

Whether it be ridiculed, travestied, or crushed beneath a heap of hostile theories, truth, when its day is come, will issue from your rubbish in all the brightness of its eternal youth; will trample under foot your accumulations of falsehoods, will look full at the sun, and the whole earth beholding her shall clap its hands.

How differently it fares with a character that is misapprehended! It lacks neither energy, nor sincerity, nor determination to defend itself at all costs. But alas! it has to defend itself alone; it is condemned before it has spoken; it is not even allowed to be what it is. A mould awaits it—like those coffins of mummies which concealed the face of the dead beneath a traditional mask—and it is shut up therein. Only, as the person thus coffined is not dead, he suffers. He also protests. Who listens to him? No one. If you were to listen to those people, there would be no end of it. The world has no time to lose; it meets you, takes your measure, judges you—a summary proceeding which perfectly satisfies it. What? shades of opinion! A conscientious analysis from the world? Why, what do you take it for?

You have blue eyes; consequently you are fair, amiable, languishing, dreamy, and insipid.

You have black eyes; you are passionate, hard, violent, obstinate.

Some flashes of enthusiasm have escaped you. Oh, I see what you are; a man, imaginative, sentimental, impressionable; adieu common sense, adieu sound judgment, don't pretend to these; bay the moon, play the guitar, and be satisfied thus.

You have, on some occasion or other, shown certain solid qualities. You! I understand you perfectly, you are a practical person. A limited and precise intellect; narrow and rigid views; healthy but small notions; there is your portrait, take it as I give it you, for no change will be made in it.

This man is a believer. He! his description is

placarded everywhere then. He is a puritan; stiff, angular, ill-favoured. He is the enemy of whatever sings and blossoms beneath the sky; he would impose silence on the birds in the bushes; order the flowers to shut up; tear the canvas of a Raphael; and break the statues of a Michael Angelo. He, he is a man of the Bible, of hell, of dark visions; with narrow brain, and heart of ice; timid, curbed, trembling, yet despotic; he is Calvin's man; he has burnt Servetus; whatever you do, beware of him.

That woman, retired and modest, glides towards the dwellings of the poor, and takes joy with her there. Oh! I have known her ever so long; why, one fold of her starched dress told me at once what she was; one of those rigidly virtuous characters lined with concealed coquetry. How much spite and longing after the world there lurks beneath her austerity! for she is austere, and somewhat hypocritical to boot; ambition beneath all that humility; the servant of the poor whom she rules; a Maintenon, in short! Or if, indeed, a divine tenderness beams from her gentle eyes, she is a Guyon, a mystic enamoured of grace. You can see her at a glance; her arms extended in the form of a cross, her eyes floating in a seraphic intoxication; good for nothing, fit for nothing; a wax figure paralysed in its niche.

Or let another have the delicacy that should belong to virtue, so that one cannot say or read anything and everything whatever in her presence. She is a prude, one of the strait-laced, a Pharisee in silken gown.

That merry creature ;—a head with no brains in it ! That liberal mind ;—crazed with modern romances ! That heart in love with retirement ;—some simpleton incapable of charming ; some unattractive person, solitary from necessity !

You have taken a part in public matters ! Then you are, a politician. Very well. Occupy yourself henceforth with the interests of the country ; discuss them ; but do not go and meddle with science, nor literature, nor art ; we cannot permit that. Your sphere is surely vast enough for you to walk in, up and down ; turn topsy-turvy if you will ; but remain in it ; no digression ; every evasion is an act of revolt, every excursion an encroachment.

The world does not willingly admit of complete beings ; rather it draws up categories, insists upon types. This is more convenient ; as soon as you get one end of a thing you get all ; class it, number it, off-hand ; the catalogue will not get revised.

The world which is idle has also its pretensions to equity ; moreover it delights in definite notions ;

as it travels fast, it requires a beaten road, and on that road it marshals stiff files of men, who must walk straight on, turning neither to the right nor the left. There is nothing like prejudice to arrange the troublesome multitude in line and order.

You say that prejudice is cruel! This comes from her being both blind and deaf. She closes her eyes that she may stab you boldly; she knows very well that if once she were to look at you, she could not do it. She stops her ears not to hear your supplications nor your cry of agony. She likes to kill without flinching, as without remorse. If, at least, she could leave you some traces of your own self! If, in destroying, she would not disfigure you! If you might remain a man amongst men, likeable, warm, cordial; if she did not transform you into a hateful object!

Have you ever experienced the surprise that the repulsion of others towards us, awakens in our hearts? You advance towards one of those fair cohorts that march through life; you are young as they are; you have a heart like theirs, impatient for work, burning with noble ardour; you love them. There they are! They stop, they turn away, they draw back their hands, shun yours, an antipathy estranges them,—they have passed by. Yes, cry to them, if you will, that appearances deceive them; that some calumny has done you wrong; that they have not even seen your face; it is much if one of them flings you from afar a mocking farewell.

And it would avail you nothing to tear out your heart, and show it to them bleeding; they would deny the heart. In vain would you open out your soul, believing, enlightened, full of fair affections; they would deny those affections, deny that life, that soul. In vain would you let them see in turn your weakness, your courage, your hopes, your fears; that essential humanity that stirs the bowels of our fellow-man. No one would move, no one answer; there is no more kindredship; you are not their brother; prejudice, that double-edged sword, has severed you from them.

Alone, misunderstood, solitary, deprived of pity, that last consolation of the unhappy, your energy declines. Forsaken by all, you grow careless of yourself. That grimacing form, that was not yours; that ugliness that you once repulsed with all the impetuosity of a rightful indignation,—you no longer struggle against them now. People will have you thus; be it so; it is thus you will die then.

The prisoner in the iron mask was less to be pitied. His bronze face stifled him indeed, but did not disfigure. His voice remained to him, and his natural features. If his individuality was incomplete, at least it was not distorted.

Prejudice deforms, betrays everything. I compare its disloyal and wicked way of procedure to the thrice holy Hermandad of diabolical memory. When the Inquisition sent a man to be burnt, it dressed him out in a disgraceful robe, and covered his head with a cap that was ridiculously hateful. Yet that was not so much after all, for the man had still eyes, still lips; he could look at other men, could speak to them; and from that moment they hated him no longer; they felt compassion for him, and as soon as he excited compassion he could die consoled. Never fear; good care will be taken to obviate that. His distorted mouth, in which a piece of wood is forced, shall frighten people, his eyes shall roll with agony, his voice shall be a voice no longer, but only a howl. Look at him now! hideous, monstrous! Can one love monsters? Rid the earth of him, and the sooner the better!

Now in this I find a perfidy against which my whole being revolts. The *San-Benito*, whatever name it bear, whatever hand may place it on, I take and tear in pieces. And now, it is once more I myself, such as God has made me, foul or fair, it little matters. Man amongst men, once more I have the right to weep, to blush, to grow pale, as they do. Perhaps as my glance meets theirs, a lightning flash will pass between us, one of those magnetic currents which strike out light. Our hands meet, the password, the mysterious sign, is exchanged: thou art of ours ; let us walk together.

And even if it be not so, if I must needs remain barred in by the lying mask, at least God sees me. God misapprehends no one ; hideous, repulsive, my false semblance disappears. Before God, I stand such as I really am, a sinner no doubt, incapable of pleasing, detestable, nay worse ; but I become myself once more ; light streams upon me, God knows me, God has sounded me, Jesus has bent over my face, Jesus cannot be mistaken !

In short, I am what I am ; and oh the good that does one !

III

WEARINESS.

NE day this autumn we were going through the fields. The mists had all lifted ; the sun had drawn them up early ; at one moment you would have said they were large transparent festoons of drapery filling immensity, then they shrank ; their light flakes, rolled into white spirals, like wool that escapes from the carder's hands, kept rising, rising, and finally losing themselves in the depths of blue. Beneath the warm sun, the woods which had only yellowing leaves, assumed those fiery tints that painters love. One could hear the flock bleating from afar ; they were nibbling in the hedge-banks at those late plants that put forth fresh shoots in October ; inexpressibly soft breezes were passing over the country, so that but for the long nights, the hurried evenings and the lingering

dawn, one might have thought that spring was
returning.

I too was looking for flowers; a periwinkle that
had mistaken the season; some of those cam-
panulas, that in June abound in the glades, or else
the chicory with its angular stalk, adorned here
and there by a blue star;—down to the pink
thistle, whose slashed and stubborn petals confront the early frosts; down to the pale lilac
scabious, the wild mignonette, dull, green, and
scentless; all that I had disdained while July was
pouring with both hands her treasures on the
earth, I now seized with delight: this is the way
with one in autumn.

And as we were walking, and the day was drawing to an end, and a whitish veil beginning to
cover the· low lands, we heard a bleat that suddenly made us turn round. It was a lamb; it was
steadying itself as well as it could upon its slender
legs, which trembled. It had got into a patch of
clover, and was trying to get at some of the more
tender sprouts amidst leaves hardened by the
white frosts; sometimes it baa'd, calling its mother,
but she was far away; I don't know where she was.
The darkness was coming on, the cold was increas-
ing with the mists of evening; the beasts that
prowl by night would soon be out; the flock had
passed on; a lamb more or less, who looks to

that? One of our party stooped, took up the lamb, and as we got near the village a peasant smiling at our capture asked :

What on earth have you got there ?

A stray lamb !

And what will you do with it ?

Give it back to its mother.

Oh, nonsense ! it can't keep up.

Cannot keep up ! All is said in those words. Woe to them who are not able to keep up with the rest !

There are such and many such in this age of ours. I know indeed that Jesus, the Good Shepherd, is ever passing by, but will they call to him ; that he would fain carry them in his bosom, but will they suffer him to do so ?

Meanwhile there they are ; the flock going on its way has lost them, and will not return to take them up. And besides, these wailing creatures, bleating continually, stopping at every step, are wearisome to the others. The strong, the healthy are in a hurry to get on ; they have something better to do than to groan over their limping companions ; those that are able to keep up will ; those that are not able will not.

And, in point of fact, if any one does not live, it is because he was not qualified for life. When once one has got to the root of the matter, and found the proper formula for expressing a fact, one is half consoled. The fact, lamentable in itself no doubt, is again seen to form part of the general scheme. What ought to live lives; what dies ought not to live. There is logic in that, nay there is common sense, and as for me I should consider the lamb who was not perfectly satisfied with this reasoning to be highly unreasonable. And by the way, I have now no longer any right to be indignant with the Spartan mode of managing these matters; nay, I am bound to approve Lycurgus dooming weakly infants to the dunghill. That custom over, which is a pity, I do not see what society loses by clearing off its incumbrances. And as to these halt and sickly ones themselves, if they have any remnant of judgment, if, I say, they have the least appreciation of their true interests, they will applaud the legislator who frees them from the anxieties of the struggle in delivering them from the misfortune of having to live.

Tocqueville, in describing our age, speaks of 'a senile consumption that one can define in no other way than as a *difficulty in living.*'

This has attacked us all.

An inexpressible lassitude weighs down our limbs. We are tired before we have begun to toil; our heads are bowed beneath an invisible yoke; ere the burden has touched our shoulders they

give way. The fact is that our age itself is oppressive. Time arrives, its hands full of business,
claims, ideas, shakes them down upon us, and
buries us beneath them. Time is no longer that
aged man with broad wings, a watch-clock hanging at his waist which went with much ado, taking
twelve good months to make the round of the sun.
Time is now an engine-driver, mounted upon the
locomotive, that he urges at high-pressure speed ;
the train follows, truck after truck laden with merchandise ; they groan and grind along the rails,
but for all that they go fast. At every station,
officials throw bales upon the stage ; they load,
unload, bring and take away ; I even think they
bring more than they take away ; and in this
general fever, beneath this accumulation, our body
which was not built for it, bends and breaks down.

The epoch is out of proportion ; between its
exigencies and our faculties there is a sort of discrepancy that wears us out. The effervescences
of modern activity have destroyed the general
harmony, and this dislocation is amply sufficient
to explain our *difficulty in living*.

Look, we will take whatever chances to come first.
Money, for example. Money is to such an extent
the ruler of the present age, that it is hardly possible to escape from its yoke. Money scorns the
quiet habits of old world wealth ; money flies here,

flies there, constructs, demolishes, makes and un-
makes positions; falls upon some in a very cata-
ract, and crushes them; deserts others, and leaves
them to starve; heaps up gold, hollows out graves,
mingles everything, confuses everything, without
order, and without plan in this age where so much
is made of it.

And as if these capricious proceedings were not
enough, it pulls the old social machine to pieces
at its will. Certain classes used to walk together;
certain parts of the edifice depended upon each
other. Money puts what was above below, and
what was below above; comes in a night, vanishes
in a morning, like, you would say, those volcanic
forces which heave up an island out of the sea at
one throe, and the next day, by only drawing
back their breath, swallow up whole districts. The
old organizations suffer not a little; the ancient
surface of society, so skilfully levelled, is made to
sink and swell at random. Strange spectacle to
the eyes, distasteful contrast to the heart.

We leave the subject of positive indigence un-
touched; that is not a sadness, but an affliction.
Let us look at those existences which, touching
on all sides the confines of wealth, aspiring with
every instinct they possess to luxury, conceal beneath false appearances the devouring anxieties
of poverty.

The family were in easy circumstances. But a cousin, perhaps a brother, makes a good speculation on 'Change or in marriage (allow me the expression), and being a good-hearted fellow, he continues to visit his relations. Wealth comes to beat with its golden waves round the walls of the modest home. They lave it without entering. Soon they will overthrow; meanwhile they sap it.

Formerly in those snug little rooms the family dreams were of giving a little party to a few friends, of taking a walk in the gardens, of spending a whole Sunday in the country when the month of May came round. They dreamed of anniversaries, of a beautiful rose-tree to be bought secretly; dreamed of a silk gown, the first, the only one, to be given to a wife on New Year's Day, after twelve months of economy. There were dreams too of charity, the best of all: of a heap of wood placed upon some hearth where the wild wind howls; of a basket of bread hidden in an empty cupboard; of pleasures devised for those who have only the monotony of their sufferings; a singing-bird to make a garret cheerful; a fine toy, with bright colours, put into little hands that never held anything but what was ugly or dirty before. Now, however, other dreams issue from the ivory gate. In these new dreams is heard the rapid stroke of the upholsterer's hammer, the metallic ring of gold piled on gold; the deafening tumult of the ball-room, and that rustling of gorgeous fabrics at a hundred francs the yard, which drowns indeed more modest voices,—the voice of love, the voice of pity, but infuses mortal vexation into the heart of other women.

As to the husband, he is no longer dreamed of at all. As to the poor, let them get on as they can; whoever remains mouth-open and empty is an idler who has not known how to fill it. To-day, to-morrow is here; we demand from them positive enjoyments, they insist upon ready money. Soon come hours of desperate searches in coffers emptied out; of debate between actual want and insatiable desire. The moral being is not only dislocated, but perverted.

Formerly it was looked upon as quite natural that there should be high positions and low. In those days people lived on where God had seen good to put them; one did one's best; some rolled in carriages, others walked. If the latter were a little splashed now and then, on the other hand they enjoyed the sunshine more thoroughly; there was happiness for every one. At the present time there is none, except at the bottom of a money-bag. When once it has come to this, why should it be he who gets it, and not I? And if I choose to have my share of pleasure, who, pray, shall prevent me? The share taken is long and wide. The man who sees his bark about to founder, puts up a fresh press of sail and capsizes. Or else he tries no expedient, merely amuses himself, and forgets all about it. Emoluments melt down in the furnace of vanity; the patrimony becomes involved, decreases. One fine day it is found that nothing short of a miracle can get the two ends to meet, and this miracle one knows will not be wrought. In becoming a heathen, one has lost the right to depend upon God. The soul, that last possession, is attainted, devoured. Evil thoughts swarm like vultures around a corpse. That which is dead may be torn to pieces without fear. The mind deteriorates; mean struggles lower its tone. The heart is empty; too much self-love has rendered all other love impossible. Nevertheless, one must go on, must keep up appearances, deceive the clear-sighted. Then it is that the fearful battle with penury begins, and one hears that cry of the panting creature, forced by the huntsman into a hopeless and pitiless race.

The rich, too, have an exhaustion of their own; it is only fair that they should. Without speaking of the aridity brought upon some by the excess of material enjoyment; without dwelling upon that foolish pride of life, foolish independence of God, which threaten all who are in high places, wealth preserves none of its favourites from the weariness of the present age. All gold mines are not in California, and rather than risk the chances of the voyage thither, many discreet persons prefer to dig and search at home. The soil where they carry on these operations is—the rich man; and each onslaught by the diggers, who set to work in a most courageous manner, shakes and reduces him.

The one exacts, the other proposes; one man borrows, another begs. Such or such an enterprise invites your capital; this or that undertaking demands your revenue. He who has been ruined by rashness, thinks your prudence cannot be better employed than in repairing his follies. He who is on the point of breaking, assures you that if you do not endanger your means, where he has lost all his, you will have his ruin upon your conscience. All eyes are fixed upon you. From every breast exhales a sigh of which you are the object. And as you are but man, not God; as in body, soul, and purse alike, you are a creature essentially limited, a being essentially finite, you become utterly discouraged and depressed. Your faculties, swamped in this torrent of solicitation, float at random. Your incapacity increases, one would say, at each excessive pretension of others:

those words of Scripture recur to your mind:
' Every one asks him, and he is grieved.'

For there are struggles too, and 'terrible questions for the rich man's conscience. Of course I
wish to give ; I shall give much, give increasingly.
But at last I must come to ask myself, in what
proportion ?

Of course I shall listen to those who implore, I
shall not harshly repulse supplicating hands ; but
can I enlarge my sphere of action so as to take in
the whole world ? And if I satisfy these, it becomes
a matter of necessity that I should dissatisfy those.

To help true poverty,—why, that is my duty and
joy ; but to throw money into that bag with holes
which idleness carries, would be to patronize the
vicious, and to defraud the deserving. Come then,
let us look into it more narrowly ; let us write, let
us run here and there; and when at length we have
decided (after how much hesitation, and what examination, ye rich Christians say), there comes a
gnawing care, there wakes a fear of having done
wrong, then an overweening anxiety about this or
that favourite undertaking. The soul grows faint,
energy slackens. If that were all! but there is worse
than that ; the heart grows cold, compassion gets
worn out, and we look on with an evil satisfaction to
the time when, the purse being empty, we may, in
all good conscience, answer, No, to every petition.

But may one indeed do this?

Harassed, broken down, over done, one goes on working at one's trade of rich man. One does this, much as the engines at the mint heap up and scatter the coin. The delights of charity are gone, spontaneous liberality has disappeared, the throbs of the heart have ceased; there are no more brotherly reciprocities. Cold lifeless fingers let fall a certain sum into a hand fevered with the craving to obtain it. The poor lose the sanctifying joy of gratitude; the rich, the free impulses of generosity.

This is indeed a weariness.

I know nothing but faith that can raise us up from it. In this whirlwind, nothing but giving our hearts completely to Jesus can enable us to find peace. The heart that has thus given itself, will just abandon whatever God chooses to take, and simply enjoy what he is pleased to leave; and as to anxieties and remorse, let us carry these instruments of torture, and lay them down before God. He has long ago abolished torture.

Whenever we feel the pincers seize us, the saws bite, and the braziers burn, it is generally because we have left Jesus, to fight all alone on the battle-field of this world.

Our generation is sickly,—another source of weariness.

I do not charge the present day with the fearful epidemics of old; but for all that, health is not its forte. Our age will never pass for a robust one. It has its energies indeed—its bursts of strength; and when it mounts the breach of a city or a pre-judice, its arm soon lays both low. But with the exception of these flashes of vigour, it is an invalid age. It has nerves; it looks with a languid eye upon the world; it is subject to fits of inexpressible debility; sometimes we have fever, sometimes palsy; one thing is certain, we have not health.

If you want strong organizations, and the gaiety which springs from a tenacious vitality well-riveted to the frame, you must look in the direction of our grandparents. They got up at early dawn, some chirping song upon their lips, just as the linnets do. They did what they had to do merrily,—not over scrupulously, I allow. They were a little given to scold men and maids; stormed away at things in general; and I do really believe that this helped to keep up their spirits.

They breakfasted well, dined well, and supped well. They managed their affairs with a high hand. They read and wrote; not too much of either; just enough to prevent these accomplish-ments growing rusty. They walked straight on firm legs; they had a florid complexion, smooth foreheads, and a ringing laugh. Such of them as

were not carried off by some scourge accomplished
the cycle of their fourscore years, with all their
faculties fresh. They knew little of doctors except
as described by Molière; and if any one had
spoken to them of neuralgia; if they had had a
glimpse of our delicacy, our feebleness, our *difficulty in living*, most certainly unbounded astonishment, with something of contemptuous irony,
would have spread over their features.

We of this generation, on the contrary, are liable
to strange fits of weariness; they come upon us
the first thing in the morning; our strength is
exhausted before our eyes are well open. Our
head droops languidly to one side. That neuralgia
at which our ancestors would have laughed, does
too surely dig its talons into our brain. Breath-
lessness seizes and stops us at every step. Who is
there that can walk now-a-days? There are indeed some who even climb, I grant you, as there
is a Mont Blanc; these are the privileged, not to
say the eccentric. The common run of mortals,
the men of the city, of the *salons*, do not walk.
One is dragged along; one drags one's-self along.
We get up late, we go to bed at dawn; and thus
we escape the sun and its vulgar brightness. We
are slender, we are pale, we are very fashionable-
looking; but decidedly we are not robust.

Robust! Why, who would wish to be anything

so commonplace ?   Robust !   Why, that is the very
triumph of matter over mind !   Robust !   Even those
women of waistcoat and paletot-wearing type
would hardly tolerate such an imputation.   Neither
our men of intellect nor the higher classes of
society would justify that epithet.

Look at those intelligent brows ; they wear the
plait of over tension.   Look at those expressive
eyes ; they are sunken, their eyelids droop a little
as if they had gazed too long.   Those lips have a
melancholy smile ; an effort has called it, an effort
keeps it there ; it lacks its pristine grace.   Even
the charm of that attractive gentleness reveals a
degree of debility ; suffering lurks beneath it ; I
guess, I feel its presence ; it gives a certain plaintive sweetness to the glance ; it trembles in the
sympathetic tones of the voice ; the perfumes that
exhale from the heart are those that can only be
obtained from bruising the plant.   Yes, it is very
true ; our generation, less loud, less vigorous than
the one that preceded it, has more of delicacy.
Perhaps I prefer these weak ones to those strong ;
my soul, in its sorrows, would find more help from
this sickly race than from that robust one.   Bad as
our health may be, we shall be found to have actually accomplished things as great as our more vigorous predecessors ; but for all that, we suffer.   A
latent passive suffering affects us night and day, and

undermines us. If in critical moments the energy of the mind be found to prevail over the feebleness of the body, in everyday life it is the reverse. The emergency finds us equal to it; the daily detail tramples us down. Now it is this very detail that is the scourge of our epoch. The chariot that moves slowly disturbs but little dust; the car that flies at full speed raises it in whirlwinds. And our age goes full speed. Each revolution of the wheels throws off, on this side and on that, men, ideas, projects, affairs; and here too, in the excessive development of a material activity, to which the growth of our powers is not commensurate, I find one great cause of weariness.

Other machines have multiplied their power tenfold; the human machine remains what it was. Nevertheless, it must keep up; the others, to whatever perfection they may have been brought, cannot as yet dispense with it; in time perhaps they may; that will be the ultimate step; but we have not taken it at present. And meanwhile the poor human machine is taken in tow; pushed, strained, put out of joint; but for all that, it must keep pace with the rest. It keeps pace, and breaks down.

If you ask for facts in proof, look, for instance, at our letter-writing! Formerly, when two people loved each other much, they wrote twice a month, and got on very well ; now, people between whom there is little love write to each other every morning, and get on no better. Formerly, mere acquaintance; nay, even lawyers required some important motive to set their pens going; now, each interest, each anxiety, takes a steel beak and thrusts it into your nerves. Formerly, the post afforded time for reflection ; one turned one's cross moods over and over in one's mind, before one gave them vent ; many a sadness had been transformed into joy during the interval between one mail and the next; many difficulties had found their solution ; people used to tell you of events when they had happened; now they write them off while they are happening.

Distance, which used to be your protection, protects you no longer ; it is one of the things the age has suppressed. Everything speaks, cries aloud, insists upon my listening to it. At every moment antagonistic individualities—some of them actually unknown—intrude upon my time, and take possession of it. Enmities or friendships, existing three hundred miles off, come to me, either to scold or caress. Twice, four times, a day these voices make themselves heard ; my life is broken up.

I am at work ; the work demands all my faculties ; some duty claims the whole vigour of my soul ;—there comes the postman !

'Take and read!' Alas! it is no longer the grave and peaceful tone that St. Augustine heard; it is a feverish injunction which agitates me.

I do take; I read; clouds gather; I feel my power fail me under these appeals that come from every point of the compass at once. Griefs upon griefs, anxieties, discontents, reproaches, requests; one is exacting; the other angry; a third comes and lays upon my conscience obligations which he has invented, comfortably sitting with his feet on the fender: Come here; go there; I shall be with you on such a day. These diverse tongues, confused as at Babel, have all one shrill note. I was full of energy; a nameless inspiration—a luminous life—had strung up my whole nature; I walked, head erect, in the healthy air; there was a good deal of work, indeed, before me, but, with God's help, proportionate to my power; I should soon have got to the end of it; now I have nothing, I am nothing, but a creature absolutely annihilated.

And then notes! how describe their worrying importunity! For a mere nothing—a yes, a no—the first idler that likes fires off a little note at me. All day long I am a mark for this practice. A mere trifle, you say! By no means; it interrupts, teases, fidgets; not to say that one has to answer! Ah yes, I too have felt the charm of writing long letters to those one loves; I know the fascination of the animated reply, when two minds give out sparks at the crossing of the blades; but there must be leisure for this; the man who is harassed by a packet of urgent missives, will never be able to allow himself the exquisite pleasure of writing as inclination prompts. No, he will take note paper of smallest size, will write his largest hand, and tell his leading facts as curtly as he can; then stuff the sheet into the envelope. Quick, fasten, stamp the envelope, then on to another, and another, till the fatigued mind hardly knows what it is about; till the paralysed fingers refuse their office; till the pen grinds instead of gliding over the paper; till, like a rebellious slave, you are seized with a frantic inclination to break the instruments of your torture, and throw out of window, inkstand, blotting-book, bundle of letters, postman, and yourself too, and so have done with it all!

But one throws out nothing whatever. A man of toil, one must needs accomplish one's task, however tedious. Besides, with an effort I shall get through it. Say it takes three hours, nay, say four. Come, let us clear out this desk once for all, and set our conscience free. Here is the heap. I vow I will not stir till I have got rid of it by legitimate means; when once that is done, I shall breathe again. The packet dwindles; only three more letters; only one; no more now. That is over! I have a vile headache, to be sure, but I don't care for that—I am free.

Then your servant gives two discreet taps at the door; enters silently; lays down on your table about a dozen notes; and retires gently, observing, The mid-day post, Sir!

And there will be an evening post besides!

Or say that you are in the country; a railroad crosses your grounds, or grazes them, or whistles at a few hundred yards from your gate.

'Dear so and so, send for me at the station of ——; I know you would take it ill if I passed you by so close without coming to see you.'

Some claim hospitality as a matter of course; others whom you do not know wish to know you; others avail themselves of the opportunity, finding themselves so near. People are constantly coming in and going out in your house. Strange faces, characters more or less congenial, drop into your home-circle, like Paixhan's balls.

That self-possession, that as it were self-intimacy without which no good is to be done, is all lost; your occupations are disturbed; your thoughts sent adrift; family life, that holy life which alone fosters character or bestows happiness, is bored through and through, and in order to recover it,

I know many who fold their tents, and take to running about like the rest of the world.

Shall I speak of telegrams! For my part I never see one of those grey envelopes arrive without a shudder. People may say what they will, they bring more bad news than good. And then these telegrams have a summary way of proceeding, which knocks one completely down. Letters alleviated the blow, or at all events they prepared for it ; they anticipated your questions, they told you what you wanted to know. The telegram either half kills you or bewilders you ; and having done that, leaves you there. I know, indeed, that in an instant, from one end of the world to the other, voices may question and answer ; rapidly disquieted, one may be rapidly re-assured. But distance and time, two instruments of torture, are also conditions of life ; they place some interval between the anvil and the hammer ; take that away, the hammer will strike without cessation, and the broken anvil fall to pieces beneath the blows. In order to breathe, man must have air ; and I question whether, in order to exist, he does not require in a certain measure both time and space ; one and the same moderating influence under two modes.

And they threaten us with a private telegraph from house to house ! The first bore who may take it into his head to ask us how we are, or to inform us that he has just sneezed, will but have to place his finger on the electric keys ; and though we be enclosed under triple bolts the lightning will strike us ! Neither the tête-à-tête, nor solitude, nor the labour of the brain, nor prayer, nor day, nor night will preserve us. When that comes, it will be all over with us indeed !

With us perhaps, but our children will live through it. Let us try to console ourselves with that idea. The present generation has to bear the brunt of the transition ; it opposes to it all the rigidity of former habits, it goes on ascribing to each of the small events that the age so rapidly throws off, that exceptional character that rarity once gave. It resembles those old people who have never got beyond the ancient coinage, and take our piece of twenty francs for louis-d'or. Everything agitates it because everything retains its importance. Do not be alarmed ; the rising generation will know how to put things in their proper places. Our ears ring, our heads are split; they will let the noise go on, will listen little, and enjoy excellent health.

Why, look at them already ! we are agitated, they keep quite calm ; what upsets us completely hardly disturbs them ; we run, they sit. Letters, electric messages, come one after another, rise, swell, smother them ; no, their indifference floats

above all. For us in our youth, action, movement was the chief enjoyment, for them it is rest.
We used to dream of travelling ; they of a comfortable stationary little life. When our fathers
wished to throw us into an ecstasy they said, I
am going, and will take you with me ! When we
want to please them we say, I am going, and I
shall leave you behind.

They will not derange themselves over much ;
they will not stir. In vain may electric wires
cross each other over their heads, despatches hiss
like bullets, letters fly like arrows ; they will keep
quiet, close their doors, counterfeit death, and do
very well.

Thus it is that the next generation will calm
down, things will be in agitation, people in peace.
The soul will regain its elasticity, the will its
empire. I think those quiet ones will do more
and better than we.

Meanwhile, here we are in the very thick of the
storm. God knows of what we are made ; all
my hope lies in that. And yet there are dispensations that leave me marvelling. Weary to death,
I try to shake off fatigue. God wills that his
people should be full of joy. I try to enjoy myself. Very little suffices ; just a flower, a day of
truce, and I am better already. But no. God

will not permit this. If I raise my head above the waves, his powerful hand presses it down again.

Anxieties were devouring me before, here comes fresh and more distressing anxiety. Faint and exhausted, I needed help, and I am knocked down by a final blow. Smothered beneath a multiplicity of duties, I wanted some leisure, and a bushel full of other business is poured out upon my head.

At the last gasp! Have you ever fully understood that expression? Do you know how deep a tragedy it implies?

The stag has been labouring hard all day long. Dogs, people, hounds full cry, horns blowing shrill, bloodthirsty fury have been pursuing him. Evening comes; his breathless course has brought him back to the fountain that in the early dew, in the silent peace of a beautiful morning he had lightly skimmed with his cool nostrils. Then worn out, feeling the teeth of the dogs meet upon his foam-flecked sides, he raises his head, gives one long bellow, and weeps.

Yet no. God is not cruel. He knows the limits of my powers; God from that height where he reigns has taken compassion upon me. A breath from above refreshes my blood; the spirit that raises the dead has placed me once more upon my feet; that spirit is life itself. I believe this; nay more, I have felt it.

The whole Bible echoes with one beautiful cry of exhortation : Trust in God. A more tender accent, the voice of him who has himself known human weariness speaks to me : Fear not ! I may wear out my mother,—Jesus will never be tired of me. When by means of care upon care God has brought me to despair utterly of myself, my faith places its foot firm on the ruins, grows into plenary power, and braces my joints anew. I throw myself just as I was at the feet of Jesus ; it is a different man that rises up ; his face is turned to the east.

My God is the God of the weary—of the afflicted ; he himself has taken that gracious name ; but when he is about to stamp the coin with the heavenly die, he puts it back into the furnace ; this is absolutely necessary ; God melts and re-melts it till the gold, made malleable, is capable of receiving the indelible impress.

A torpor has seized me ; the lethargy of sadness. Let others break out into indignation against the sleep of the Apostles in the Garden of Olivet ; I, for my part, cannot do so. The crushed soul has these fits of somnolence ; the extreme of lassitude has its magnetism.

Hunters tell us that the lion's claw, laid upon a man, throws him into a kind of delirious sleep ; he sees everything, not one horrible detail escapes him; but for all that he does not move; his active faculties have vanished; motionless as in a dream, he endures, he looks on, as it were, at the drama, like a paralysed spectator.

Our fatigue lays the same malignant claw upon us.

Before the morning has whitened the sky, we shrink from it; it is the re-commencement of life; a distaste and a distress come upon us; our eyes are scarcely open when our spirits sink; discouragement and *ennui* pounce upon us; the cords are relaxed, the spring is worn out; crushed beneath the pressure of a rude hand, the delicate instrument has ceased to respond. The sorrows of the world rise to the heart like poisoned exhalation from a swampy plain; all things present their gloomy side to our view. But there is worse than this. They that suffer feel; we feel no longer. Nothingness opens its yawning abysses, from whence issues the corroding question, To what purpose? The moment these words, occurring to the soul, suspend at a point of interrogation a sentiment, a duty, or a pleasure, it is all over, and what they have once poised in the balance soon falls into the abyss.

Nothing affects me any more, and I no longer affect any one. I become indifferent to myself.

Alas! it is too true, there are people who lose all self-interest through very incapacity to be interested in anything. Tired of all alike, without regrets, without desires, they can neither rejoice nor grieve. The mirror has lost its polish ; images are reflected no longer ; dust obscures the very sun. Is there indeed a sun ? of what use is it if its rays are deadened ? Joy no longer cheers ; happiness bestows nothing ; and to give the climax to this miserable condition, our angry conscience points to a future full of threatenings. 'Thou shalt regret then ! What then thou wilt have lost, shall give thee the measure of thy present possessions !'

I know it but too well, and that the day is coming when these slighted treasures, for ever removed, will appear to me in all their wondrous beauty, and that the prism will have all its colours, and that it will be too late. I know this, and remorse completes my wretchedness.

We have come to the worst effect of weariness, —incapacity. It is because it renders us incapable that weariness does us such cruel wrong.

Wide as the distance between heaven and earth is that which separates a submissive acceptation from the inertness of an incapacity to resist. He who has faith in his own powers will soon stand up again ; he who knows himself incapable, will not even make an effort.

And, singular fact! acuteness of vision increases in proportion to impotence of will. The greater the atrophy of the active faculties, the clearer grow the perceptions. The vital energy which has retired from the heart, concentrates itself upon the analytical powers of the mind, excites and exasperates these, and this fresh discord brings on additional debility.

Incapable! I have not always been so. I was advancing in my youth, full of energy and full of hope; I heard within me, as it were, the gushing of living waters; I was liable to enthusiasms, indignations; no obstacle daunted me; I felt myself capable of defying giants. Life came, broke, dislocated, melted me down.

Do not talk to me of admiration. How can I admire? how get breath enough? Admiration soars in lofty regions, I creep. To admire? why, it is to create! Is there the creative material in an over-driven being? Easy delights, fresh, innocent surprises, belong to the strong. I am a valetudinarian; I see what invalids see, the negative side of everything; I criticise, my remnant of life takes that outlet; it is the senility of the soul; I tell you I am a hundred years old!

That I should wax indignant? Wherefore, pray, and for what? Ask the horse, exhausted by the charge, whether he has the strength to rear?

Happy they who retain generous indignations; they who cannot hear, without turning sick at heart, the public crier in the Southern States of America announcing the sale of his human merchandise; they who cannot behold, without their conscience protesting, the lash of the gendarme threatening the Christians who read their Bible in Spain. Happy they whom the age has not so utterly worn, but that they still retain noble angers and ideal loves. As for me, those sorrows and those joys, those unsightly and those magnificent objects, alike leave me inert; I perceive them, indeed, but they cannot succeed in electrifying me. I have fallen into everyday life, everyday opinions; I contribute my relay of labour, I contend with the storm; as soon as I have arrived I set off again, always on the same road, always under weight. Why do you come and speak to me of a gallop on the steppes,—of a 'fantasia' in the Desert? Address yourself to the coursers of Arabia; the bridle does not make their mouth bleed; their sides are not torn by the spur; they may fly over the free expanse, if you will; as for me, I trot in harness.

Inferior in all things, trial finds me below its requirements; but happiness still more. What God demands I am unable to give; what men expect from me—faith, sympathy, refreshing cheerfulness—I have not got. I can plainly see that they go away from me disappointed, just as they would turn from a spring that has dried up. Even those whom I love, and who love me, I fail to render happy; my lassitude depresses them; my weaknesses exhaust. I am not to any of them, nay, not to this one, not to my chief treasure even, either a cause of joy or an element of progress. His intellectual life owes me nothing; his heart-life little more. Were I gone—the first explosion of grief over—nothing essential would be taken away from him; nay, perhaps he would but breathe the more freely—perhaps he would be conscious of a degree of relief. I am like those dead branches which encumber the tree, and check fresh vegetation. People find me disagreeable, troublesome, useless. I own that they are right; but what of that? this does not tend to improve me; rather the sentiment of incapacity—the only persistent one I have—makes me awkward, and gives me an unpleasing hesitation. Through feeling myself tiresome, I become so; through believing in my want of power, I remain powerless and supine before those enemies of our happiness that I ought to have wrestled down. The evils that I might have overcome devour their prey under my very eyes; I do not even act as a scarecrow!

To see suffering, and to be conscious of one's

own inanity, this is indeed the dregs of the bitter cup.

But shall we remain in this plight? Stretched out on the sands, shall we say, Here I will die?

God wills not our death; that were too easy. God wills that we should live, and that we should be happy!

I have said much of Divine help; one cannot say too much. I now appeal to human energy. God demands athletes; he gives strength to the strong—Air! Room! If these are refused you, take them by force.

Do not let us act like those Indians—the legitimate possessors of America—who let themselves be driven back by the invaders, decimated by the fire-water, and who retreat, diminished, silent, till, effaced from one spot after the other, there is not a trace of them left upon the soil that God had given them. Our time is our own; our family life our own; the right to breathe; the duty to work is inalienably ours. There is one Master, God; I know no other. So much the worse for the men who allow themselves to be tyrannized over by their fellows.

Would you re-conquer vigour of soul; would you achieve anything good or great?—belong to yourself, possess your existence, have your own hours. Acting thus, you will not be cruel to others, far otherwise; a heart will be born again within your breast, and you will give it.

The locomotive crushes with perfect indifference things, animals, or men. The excess of activity gives us something of the same character; it is when one obeys a mechanical impulse that one destroys everything on one's way. Let us beware of having neither time to be kind, nor time to be human. He who insists upon his leisure will have sympathies; the man who makes himself an engine will be hard as iron.

Have no fear of belonging too much to yourself. If I was persuading you to cross your arms to live at ease, the counsel would be diabolical; but I want you to give yourselves, to give yourselves indeed, to give yourselves to Him whose you should be; and we can only give what we really have. You cannot! The hour is passed! There is no renewing our youth. God can renew it, if only you are willing.

Some one once said, 'I am accused of believing in human will. I believe in it, because I believe that human will is God's grace.' 'And,' added that woman, for the speaker was a woman of high intellect and large heart, 'no one will ever persuade me to the contrary: those who say I cannot, are those who think I will not.'

IV

DECAY.

YOU have seen, have you not, on some of the tombs that ancient Rome scattered over the Campagna, those processions of veiled women, each of them carrying some funeral urn, pressed against her breast. It is thus we too walk; the most frivolous amongst us embrace a funeral urn holding ashes. Destruction accompanies every vital process, and conquers life at last. In all cases, it is only upon the conditions of losing that we can ever acquire.

Ruins do not sadden all people, and without counting those dreamy souls who prefer memories clinging with the ivy round the walls of an old tower, to the glaring prosperity of the modern castle, I know a good many whom demolition amuses. I go further, I say whose pride it gratifies. He who watches an overthrow, compares it complacently with his own stability ; he who destroys anything may easily imagine himself strong.

I do not belong to this class. All decay seems to drag with it a part of my own life. Ruins ! The word, like a pebble thrown into a pit, strikes at different depths, and makes me appreciate the abyss. Unless the eternal youthfulness of nature clothes the dismantled walls, the gaps in them sadden me.

I was sauntering beside the borders of the forest not long ago. A small house threw open its windows there ; children played round the door ; hollyhocks stood out against the dark green of the oaks, and when one entered the enclosure, the noises from the cow-house, the mother telling the little ones to be good, the father loading his cart with tiles, the neighing of the old horse, the water gurgling in the fountain, all told of happiness. Now all is gone. A tragedy occurred in the retired nook. Justice has thrown the father into prison ; the mother is dead ; the children have left the country; the dwelling which had become an object of horror has disappeared, has indeed been completely razed. The plough has passed over the ground, and left its uniform furrows there. Only upon the accursed site, half buried beneath a heap of stones, one beam projects, and the very sight of it makes one shudder. The whole house deserted and shut up, with seals on the doors, would not have affected one so much; the field, with its crop all starred by corn-flowers and poppies, might have stifled the wail of the past beneath the magnificent hymn of spring and nature's abundance; but that one solitary beam, witness of the devastations of life and the stains on memory, that mere bit of half-charred wood, that it is which freezes one's blood.

More than one existence has some of these mute vestiges of a vanished happiness; fragments float upon the calmed-down water, that tell of the horror of the casualty that once occurred there; and at sight of them the cry of the shipwrecked mounts once more from the bosom of the ocean, and sends its wail along its fair and laughing surface.

This is an early experience; from his first steps man comes into collision with ruin. Look at the child standing stupefied before its broken toy; that makes you smile; what of that? you ask. That is the despair of your whole existence; that is a destruction.

People laugh at the soap-bubbles which burst in the air; I never could feel the gayer for looking at them. Very fragile was the skiff, a balloon! —the more fool he who trusts his fortune to it. Yes! but that little light and puny thing had in it

the force which raises above the earth ; it soared,
and then the magic prismatic colours shone on its
brittle crystal ; and it carried up along with it,
my fancy, my thought, my soul,—all within me
that craves for space and light, all that seeks
to soar.

The mortifications of a poor author who has
been hissed may divert the prudent man ; he for
his part could never think of risking his peace
upon the fate of a page of scribble.   The man
who has the good sense to live contented with
prose, laughs heartily at the mischances of the disappointed poet.   Every shower pleases the citizen
who is snugly shut in ; let the hail shrivel the
April buds as it will ; let the frost endanger the
coming harvest ; he for his part is not cold, his
fire burns brightly, his dressing-gown, properly
wadded, preserves him from draughts ; howl ye
north winds, come back winter, he laughs at you,
and positively it is a pleasant excitement to him
to look at the figure those blackened shoots cut,
and at those shivering people with their poor pale
discomfited faces.

Laugh if you will, but ruin is at the bottom of
it all, the ruin that will one day or other mock at
your destruction.

Is it absolutely necessary to be a poet in order

to be disappointed ? Alas ! it suffices to be twenty years old !

I have seen young brows lit up with a secret hope; I have met eyes in which infinite aspirations float ; everything is unknown, everything is possessed. Just because one has nothing one has all. What can seem hard of attainment to one who has measured neither opposing difficulties nor his own powers ? The little child when it sees a star sparkle, stretches out its dimpled arms ; it wants that star. To want a star is the beautiful insanity of the young. In fact, they who have never suffered from this disease will grasp nothing, not even a glow-worm. Accordingly, they want the star, these newcomers just born into existence, and already a sigh of sadness escapes their lips. Like the blind man who, even before his groping hand has met the walls, shudders and draws back, the obstacles with which they have not yet come into collision throw a chill shadow over them, and make them tremble.

Then again, the more innocent the heart, the more storms it encounters ; a worn-out heart is paralysed ; where death has passed, there is no longer any stir. Strong to feel, the young spirit is weak to react ; passions rule supreme there ; the will like a helm without a pilot obeys every casual hand. Then come terrible shocks ; the vessel sometimes rises against the wave, sometimes sinks in the trough of the sea. Generous impulses, noble indignations, enthusiasms, splendid dreams, come in turn to fill our sails. We believe the sea to be clear, the horizon boundless, the day interminable, all winds propitious, and we go and run full sail upon a rock. Some sink at the first shock, others recover. The waves wash over the deck, encumbered with broken masts, stained sometimes with the weeds and mud of the shallows ; the sea is taken again, dejectedly, without any flourish of trumpets now. Some navigators, with long voyages before them, become coasters, and hug the land ; others with their damaged craft dare mid-ocean, for if tempests lurk in the deep waters, there are shoals and breakers near land ; everywhere there is danger, everywhere destruction.

Thus it is that the soul wounds itself by contact with reality ; surprises fraught with bitterness lie in wait for it ; its discoveries are marked by bursts of grief. Like the prisoned butterfly that, seeing the daylight through the panes of glass, dashes against them again and again, and at each shock loses the bloom upon its wings, so the young man sees the sky, aims at it, and every fruitless effort leaves him bruised. Besides, this painful reality is a force ; it keeps youth in check ; those who govern the young have acknowledged its rights; they have had to bend, they insist upon others bending. This is good in a measure; but if carried too far, it lacerates and crushes. The difference between the two temperatures, so to speak, gives birth to the hurricane. The rolling floods of lava meet the cold in-flowing tide of the sea; a hissing shriek rends the air, clouds of vapour rise, one would say that the ocean would be dried up; but no, after this great conflict all grows still; cold has conquered.

Perhaps that youth over-indulges its emotions, exaggerates its desires; on the other hand, maturity too often impoverishes life; it takes a sort of pleasure in widening the wounds of disappointment. By the side of the Eden where God's creatures were walking in the liberty of their ignorance, it likes to spread out arid plains, where weary travellers bent and bleeding go. The youthful soul, cut to the quick, like a fiery steed by an unskilful trainer, becomes exasperated, and protests with all the strength of its rebellion against the rude opponent that would subdue it.

How many there are in arms against our early sorrows! Sometimes satire surprises our sacredly veiled secret; sometimes the impossibilities of practical life rear themselves in our path. Never! That word, so terrible to us at twenty, sinks down

upon the heart ; and if that heart will not submit,
it breaks it !

Next there comes the knowledge of evil. Pitfalls
yawn, ugly objects appear, hideous spots, where
before we saw the sky ; an up-turning of the soil
of the heart of which none but God must know.

Nor is this all ; but we are watched by malevo-
lence as well. One was moving on with a smile
upon the lips, and eyes tearful with sympathy ;
to love seemed just as natural as to breathe.
Suddenly one discovered that there were people
who thought otherwise,—people who did not love.
The hand that we had stretched out is drawn
back trembling ; we are not liked, nay, we are
disliked ; what harm can we have done ? We do
not know ; destruction is at work there.

There are looks that poison, words that ruin,
there are destroyers among those who breathe
our air.

And thus life wears on. At each loss we believe
that we have lost all ; nevertheless we shall suffer
again, suffer always ; and disappointment, by dis-
sipating our dreams, will demonstrate to us with
certainty, that we had continued to indulge in
them.

Shall I speak of plans, of castle-building, that
poor, little, everyday thing? Plans ? Why, they are
the very Genius of the Lamp, who suddenly makes

his appearance in our commonplace existence, with his giant stature and his attitude of slave. You invoke him, powerless as you are, and there he is ! Distant shores are brought near; you wander beneath the palm-trees of the Nile ; your foot treads inaccessible mountain summits ; the waves of the Bosporus rock you reclining in your galley; or else it is your bride, radiant yet timid, that comes to cross your threshold. Your very home extends like a tent whose curtains are stretched out ; that fountain bursts forth beneath your beech-trees ; that forest opens out to you its perfumed glades. Industrial enterprise had built its fortresses between you and the view; the genius sweeps them off in a morning, and again you see the valley, and the windings of the river dividing the meadows by their line of white. Yes, but the genius deserts you ; his form, indistinct like smoke, trembles a little, evaporates; and when ruin has invaded these domains of fancy, oh how denuded the house seems, how grey the sky, how contracted the heart !

I hate discouraging words; they take away from us even the desire of overcoming evil. And yet if lamentations enervate us, illusions lead astray, nothing but the truth can really restore us.

The heart amused by cheats and shams remains

inert. Never will such a one, suffering from an immense want of happiness, go and ask for it from Heaven. It is the man who has known the grasp of grief who feels the wakening of an inward power. Dragons make the Hercules. People may laugh at the disproportion between our ideas and reality, but it is just here that I find the first step of the ladder which leads up to the regions of light.

Besides, the blows that he receives fortify the athlete ; if we are never to be beaten, we must never go to battle. Rather the wounded warrior than the idler intact !

And again, did what experience has deprived us of deserve so many tears ? Are we very sure that bereavement has ruined us ? In the moral world we possess only what we have gained. A little faith is worth more than much presumption ; a little love for the Saviour is better than the fruitless ecstasies of mystical tenderness. I prefer a little energy to all the flourishes of the declaimer.

There is a sublime expression in one of the Gospels ; the Baptist who had been shaking the whole population of Judea, made use of it when his disciples, whom he had just sent to Jesus, re-turned exclaiming, ‘ Master, he baptizes, and all men go to him.’ Then said John, ‘ He must increase, and I must decrease.’

When the work of destruction has taken place, and nothing is growing under the ruins, death indeed is there. When the demolished stones, rolling away to right and left, make room for the vigorous oak, there is life. Life pushes away and overthrows inanimate things. Decay, did you say, was here? No! It is rather youth, and the eternal forces of nature.

But these begin by destroying.

Who has not dreamed of an easy royalty? In fact, man is born a king; there is always some sceptre and some crown concealed in the curtains of the cradle; ask the mother if it be not so. Poet, legislator, man of science, leader of armies; look at them closely,—you will see the rattle.

And so one advances, a halo round the brow, a globe between the hands. These hands are still weak, but they do not tremble. A *Te Deum* rises around the young sovereign. The monarch is frank, has all the grace of good princes, all their generous trust. What is this? A murmur! Some one has shrugged his shoulders; a levelling finger has been pointed at the royal robe, a clamour has risen, a shout of ridicule been heard. He looks at himself, at others;. others shake their head! Then he uneasily asks himself, who is right; which speaks true, they or I? It seems to himself, indeed, that he holds a golden sceptre, that a diadem girds his head, that the purple floats round his steps. Is it indeed the purple? The supreme fall of falls, mark you, is this, the first doubt of one's-self.

And yet if the sapping process has not laid our presumption low, firm faith, productive faith, will never come. For this faith needs a soil that has been deeply ploughed. The wind carries away the light seeds thrown on the surface of the fields; a creative faith requires a rending, and to sink down into the very bowels of the earth.

Meanwhile anxious questionings succeed each other. If, indeed, I were mistaken all the time? if I had only a puerile ambition? if my vanity were the one exceptional thing about me? if my mother had deceived herself? if indifferent people were to prove right? if I had been decidedly mad hitherto? if my lot should prove merely an obscure, ridiculous, useless existence.

Jesus delights to walk in these desert and desolated places; it is here that he meets with disappointed souls, whom illusory visions have forsaken.

The miner at the bottom of his dark shaft, if he looks up to the sky, can see the shining of the stars that the mid-day radiance hides from our eyes. He follows their wondrous march; those constellations that display themselves in all their magnificence ravish his soul. And we, too, from out the abyss into which disappointment has thrown us, can behold the glories of the celestial city. The hand of man has torn the human scheme to pieces; the Divine plan now appears; Jesus unfolds it to our gaze. And do not suppose that it disgusts us with this life, that heaven seen from so near diverts the labourer from his task; on the contrary, he will but buckle to it with fuller energy, and show you that it is God alone who can make men.

But we are bound to admit that humility, that force so easy to the conqueror, is far from being easy to the conquered. The good opinion of others affords us a measure of our unworthiness; their contempt, which places us below the level, naturally rouses our self-assertion to restore an equilibrium. When we are quite sure to be contradicted, there is some sweetness in thinking poorly of ourselves, nay, in speaking in that tone; when we are convinced that no one will dispute the point, we are reluctant to proclaim an inferiority too generally allowed.

The kicks of the ass may inflict a serious injury; the wit with which our blunders and mishaps inspire fools makes ugly wounds; those that cannot contrive to construct, revenge themselves by demolishing.

I can point out other ravages.

Look at that man, the man of an idea. As soon

as his intelligence woke, it grew enamoured of this idea, which is beautiful, which is true, and which was not known before he tore away its veil. He has promoted it, at the cost of much toil, sometimes of much suffering; he has sacrificed his career for its sake, has borne many sarcasms, been pointed at long—he and his idea—with a smile and a gesture of contempt. But at length, by his zeal, the idea has taken its proper place,—say it is a theory, or if you will, a privilege, a liberty. At length, behold it resplendent! And now that it is crowned, every one prizes the honour of belonging to its suite. It has its adorers, its champions, one day its victories; and that day, perhaps, its first devotee, who found it in the desert solitary and despised, who watered it with his blood, to whom it owes life and dominion,—that man lost in the crowd, insignificant amongst the insignificant, will follow its triumph afar off. No one will remember him, no one will pronounce his name, even the ridicule of which he was the object will be forgotten; all the deep waters of oblivion will pass over him; not one wave will cast up his memory. Here it is human ingratitude that plays the destructive part. A bitterness steals over the heart that is thus overlooked, a species of disgust seizes hold of it; egotism, when trampled down, rears itself to its fullest stature; then the spirits sink;

apathy casts its shadows over all,—what is the use of working more ?

Thus life in its alternations takes from us whatever it had given. Like those capricious streams that now deposit a fertilizing layer, and now sap and sweep their banks away, it enriches us or it devastates. The world clapped its hands at the beginning of our career, it extolled our courage, and loved us for our enthusiasm ; but, strange to say, one added excellence disenchanted it. That act of generosity that it had not reckoned upon offends ! it had called us chivalrous, now it pronounces us unwise ; one noble action more, and we should be Don Quixote himself !

Or this may happen by the simple up and down of the human see-saw; people had been enchanted with us, and they grow tired. Having been raised very high, we are now let fall from that height very low. Perhaps, indeed, we ourselves, without any one interfering, contrive to get some ridiculous tumble in the sight of the world ; and that world, whose favourite we had been, instead of compassionating us, breaks out into diabolical mirth. But this too is our fault ; people should not let themselves fall.

Wherever my glance wanders I see ruins. This blow knocks down part of a wall ; that, the whole building. Habit, interest, even work, even thought,

—all crumbles away. We wander amidst the debris, we search there; for what? our souls! and if we obstinately persist in trying to find these amidst the ruins; if, lifting up both arms to the Lord, we do not ask him for that spirit of life that comforts and quickens, we remain destroyed.

Happiness deceives us. This has been so constantly said that I have a great mind to assert the very contrary.

No! happiness does not deceive us; it is really happiness; it is indeed that glorious blue sky that floods us with light; it is indeed the sun. Only, who is there that has happiness? Happiness deceives no one; but she does not allow herself to be caught, that is all. Whoever touches her thinks that he has grasped her. Yes, the hem of her garment, a ray, a perfume, a harmony; and while I open my hands, enraptured, to contemplate my prize, happiness, with one strong wing-stroke, has fled away. If I want to regain her, I must mount after her, from sphere to sphere, all my life long, and it is only my last sigh that will bestow happiness herself upon me.

It is grief that deceives us, deceives us far more than happiness does; for grief we do indeed possess; and grief, though fulfilling her threats, fails to keep her promises.

We had often dreamed of grief; she had the beauty of all truly great things; the sublimity of the infinite; she was an abyss, but the ocean too has abysses which reflect, while softening them, the azure and the smile of the sky. Grief advanced like a tragic queen; she held a dagger; tears were in her eyes; her melancholy form spoke of despair; and yet what majesty in her bearing, what an austere beauty in that face, all-indifferent to the impression it made! Grief walked with royal steps; the very folds of her robe fell with a stern grace; her voice, even through its sobs, raised noble emotions; and our spirit, thirsting and sighing after immensity, opened out with a thrill to receive the divine guest.

For it seemed as though one must needs wax greater through grief—as though, to enclose it, the breast must expand. Does not the plunging deep in sorrow give that smarting delight of the swimmer who cleaves the waves with daring strokes? He disappears beneath the flood, he sinks till his foot touches the ocean bed; then he rises with one spring, and again defies the billows and defies the abyss.

Let sorrow come alone, in its proud and lonely unity; let it attack us with the sword, we will not fly! To measure ourselves against it will be to win our spurs. It is not thus that sorrow does come; it makes use neither of the lance nor the battle-axe; too often it shrinks to mean proportions, and takes vulgar tools to torture instead of knightly weapons to wound us. Extreme sorrows have not even the privilege of their magnitude; they do not keep that prerogative which seemed necessarily theirs,—of filling the heart entirely, annihilating minor griefs, and ruling the life. It is with them as with clean flesh-wounds, from which a healthy blood at first escapes; these may make you shudder, but they do not disgust you. Wait a little, the festering stage will come; you turn away your head; your heart rises against the sight.

Happy they who can receive the simple blow at the feet of Jesus! Happy they who, concealing their suffering, can bear it away out of the reach of the destroyers, and preserve to it that celestial reflex it wore when coming first from the hands of God. But no, human eyes have found it out; it is torn from us, exposed to light; each one wants to manage it in his own way. And besides, a train follows close upon its steps; a train unworthy of it, that you had not noticed at the first. Small annoyances; vexatious stings; this varlet band sets upon you; and he who had borne the shock of the colossal athlete succumbs to the blows of the vulgar herd.

Everything gets complicated. For a moment

H

you were left to yourself; your sorrow possessed
you, and you possessed it; and in that mutual
absorption, you felt the solemn calm that accompanies all contact with the infinite. Now that hour
is over. Heaven had drawn too near. Earth
claims her liege once more. You thought that
your suffering belonged to yourself; you had pur-
chased it, you said, with your life; you are in
error, your suffering is public property; throw the
doors open, let in the throng. Here come consolations, claims, and sometimes remonstrances.
One finds that you weep too much; another, that
you do not weep enough; a third, that there
should be no weeping at all. If a few bring you
the exquisite balm of those sympathies which
know how to pray and how to keep silence,
the many impose on you, at random, the com-
plications of their own minds, or the peculiarities
of their character.

This mother has seen depart the coffin of a first-
born son; the men who are bearing it, are bearing
away her joy, her hope, perhaps her daily bread.
She does not understand why God has stricken
her; but at least one consolation remains, God is
Love; if she did not believe this, she would not
only die, but her whole exasperated being would
blaspheme. Well, there are destroyers—I can call
them by no other name—who come and bid her,

with their sententious voice : ' Examine yourself;
hidden faults draw down the divine wrath ; repent
of your sins, which have killed your son.'

'Alas ! no doubt I am a sinner. If God were
extreme to reckon with me, he would kill all my
children. But you lie ; God is not that merciless
avenger that you give him out. He is not that
unpitying calculator who cuts off a limb at every
act of disobedience. God has taken my child
because he loves him. God, who loves me, is
preparing me for eternity.' So speaks the mother.
But for all, the corrosive words have worked,
penetrated, affliction has lost its beauty. You will
no longer see that woman weep upon her knees,
given up entirely to her sorrow and her faith. She
agitates and consumes herself by painful questionings. And if some one else, to finish the work
begun, comes to put before her imagination a con-
templative void, instead of a heaven throbbing with
life ; if they tell her that she will not see her son
again, that Paradise is closed against human affections ; if, instead of that Father's house, where the
mother meets once more the child of her prayers,
you stretch out before her desert spaces that all
your diffuse light can never warm,—then, wild
with despair, no longer recognising her sorrow, no
longer able even to grasp it ; banished from the
regions of the blest, flying from. the misery that

overwhelms her, she will wander, like those accursed of antiquity,—a fold of her mantle cast
over her head, her hands raised in protestation
against an implacable sky, alike far from man and
far from God.

In these peaceful hours, however, we are sometimes our own worst enemies. A destroyer works
in the gloom of our souls. Simple suffering is not
a gift given to all the world.

Our sorrow is respected, no indiscreet glance
has profaned it, no discordant utterance jars upon
our ears,—when, lo! some one begins to speak
within us. What no one would dare to say, that
speaker says. In his horrible audacity he lays his
hand upon everything; he proposes problems; he
stirs unclean depths, dries our tears beneath a
fiendish breath, dissects us alive, doubts, sneers,
decries; and you may take my word for it, if God
does not silence it, that dread voice will thoroughly
ruin and desecrate our sorrow.

Then there is another thing; the trivialities of
life are all let loose upon the broken heart. There,
where some great sorrow has smitten, clouds of
vulgar cares come swooping down like vultures.
A complete overturning of the former existence;
habits broken up; questions about money,—what
not? Joy is lost, strength is lost, and now that the
only possible solace would be to retain one's sor-

row, one must needs part with that too. Anxieties come, which push it from its place ; consolations that are worse than death. A fortune, additional luxuries, and there we are cheated, and in a manner comforted. The decay of grief, when it is brought about by selfishness, has for its characteristic, a supreme degradation.

At other times, without any agency from without, any effort of our own or of others, this giving way happens of itself. Grief totters beneath its own weight, the heart that was not strong enough to bear it, is crushed, lets it escape through all its fissures, and we remain stupefied, and as it were indignant at this overthrow.

Let us raise our heads once more, I pray you.

You do not see the hand of God in these devastations ; but for all that, it is there. Ah ! I too have known what it is to have suffering, like an enchantress skilled in deceit, administering to me her philter. The poison was blending with my blood ; my arteries were ceasing to beat. God would not have me poisoned. Shock after shock comes to wake me ; I resist them. I pray thee suffer me to sleep ! Not so, thou shalt not sleep ; thou shalt struggle and shalt overcome !

God destroys nothing, He but transforms. Such desertion of grief is horrible in his sight, as in ours.

God does not deny the existence of suffering. He never annihilates it, and never complicates it. Amongst the ruins that our feet have been trampling, there were ravages like those wrought by the destroying hand of barbarians. God does not approve of such. Only we are in a place of probation; many a chrysalis shell must fall off before we can traverse the expanses of the air. Sorrow must disclose to us its vanity; our own heart must reveal its impotence. God must re-create for us a grief, even as He re-created a soul. It is only the Christian who is capable of mourning long, mourning with a heart at once submissive and energetic, and all vibrating with hope.

Meanwhile the destroyer is abroad; he violates all sanctuaries, and now he even dares to touch our love.

Absence! what! weep for such a trifle as that? we saw each other; we do so no longer, we shall again: a fine thing to make a fuss about. But shall we indeed see each other again? Is that then so certain? And even if it were, the days spent in absence from what one loves, are lost days; they can never be brought back; they are destroyed!

This morning I possess him; I hear his voice; the sound of his step tells me that he has not left our home. If any uneasiness assail me, he is near;

if some sad mood should seize me, some terror
of a last separation, I tell him of it. Then he, with
his sweet glance, re-assures me, even laughs at my
terrors, gently chides me ; he will not let me be
fearful ; he bids me have more trust, for that God
protects us. To-morrow he will be there no longer.
I shall not hear him. Silence will have replaced
the joyous stir of life. The voice that struck upon
our walls will have vanished ; they will not even
have kept an echo of its tone. I may go with
my heavy heart all round our empty home, it will
not give him back. Now then come, gnawing
cares ; come, sudden terrors ; fall upon me at your
will, there is no longer any one to defend me !

But absence has taken nothing from me ; and
yet tenderness has decayed. So long as you keep
possession of the heart, you have all ; absence cannot interfere with that ; it is when the heart forsakes you that destruction begins.

No outward event has come into collision with
your love, but for all that your love grows pale.
The one you love breathes beside you, your dress
sweeps him as you pass ; and yet you are more
separated than if the ocean rolled its depths between you. In the pride of your affection you
thought to scale heaven, and, look ! all at once, a
confusion of tongues has come to pass ; you no
longer understand one another ; you speak in

different idioms, a discord, a false note thrills through the air. Instead of love it is indifference that replies to you ; instead of sympathy, it is sometimes anger. Then both of you are silent, each flies off in his isolation, as of old the families of men took contrary ways across the desolate plains of Mesopotamia.

And this division of souls may take place without a word being exchanged. The hardness of the glance, the impassibility of the features shocks and repels; a rending asunder goes on, without its ever being verbally noticed. Absence is nothing compared to this departure of the heart. You were wont to run to meet the beloved being ; your very soul flew forth to welcome his coming ; now the greeting is dull, a species of impatience reveals itself in his manner ; your emotions are frozen up. One is reminded of those mists that rise into a cool stratum of the air, soon to re-descend in flakes of snow. The charm has vanished ; one feels no longer the desire to please ; of what use is poetry now ? why make fruitless efforts ? that which is to go will go, do what you will. No abyss hollowed out by time, no expanse that distance can unroll, can equal those arid steppes that may all at once stretch out between two human hearts.

And the horrible thing is that when once it has come to this, chance meetings, intimacy, are all alike in vain. One dreads them, they but divide further instead of re-uniting. You are disagreeable because you are no longer loved, whatever you say, you say ill; your language, the sound of your voice, the expression of your eyes, all do you disservice, because all betray. If you weep, your tears are a reproach; his pride is irritated by them, it dries up those tears; the fear of displeasing makes you unpleasant; burning all the while with love, you are so subjugated by constraint—your face is stony, like the head of Medusa it petrifies.

We have wandered, have we not, in these labyrinths, in which, take what path we would, we were sure to go wrong. Like those hapless ones whose tortures have been described to us by a master-hand, the quicksands had got hold of us, each movement only made us sink the deeper. And just as they saw the great radiant sky and the flocks of birds of passage on the wing, so we contemplate our happiness which hovers and balances itself for a moment over our heads before it takes flight for ever.

A worse sorrow still has reached me. The heart of the one I love, frozen towards me, has learnt to beat for another. In his languid glance, another can rekindle the light. His voice had these same sweetnesses the day he first told me

that he loved me ; his forehead had the same
sudden pallor; it was thus he trembled then ; thus
that his face, as it is doing now, would light up
with happiness.   That I should complain of this !
Would I even own that I suffer?   What am I henceforth ; by what means could I possibly please him?
He does right to forsake me ; there is nothing in
me any more that can deserve to be loved.   Let
him go where his heart leads him !

Oh, beware !   A morbid pride might induce us
to leave the destroyer undisturbed at his work.
A species of inertia akin to humiliation might dispose us to put up with this.   But such resignation
is desertion ; such discouragement is cowardice ;
these are devastations that God does not will.

Our sighs which cannot reach the ears of man,
rise up to move the heart of God.   Let us not
fear when the earth shakes, and the mountains are
cast into the midst of the sea.   God is the Lord.

The horror of these convulsions is just this, that
which ought not to have failed us does fail.   The
sailor embarking, knows well the deceitfulness of
the sea he ventures on ; the soldier who enlists is
perfectly aware that bullets kill ; the pilgrim trusts
the soil he treads.   The earth, this solid genial
earth, this mother earth of ours, can it indeed open
and devour !   I had such full confidence !   The
mountains might have crumbled, my heart would

not have been cast down. But his love, his, hers! we who have wept together, have prayed, have hoped!

Hope on, hope ever, believe me this is the only way to triumph over the destroyer.

Do you remember the *Miserere* in the Sistine Chapel? At each verse a light is put out, the chant wails on, the sadder as the darkness grows deeper. It is just so; an affection, a faculty, happiness, sorrow, all disappears. Man, sitting in the unpeopled night, laments, turns back to watch the fair images which are fading one by one away. Then when all the lights are quenched and gone, and when the darkness, settling down, no longer lets us catch even a few flitting forms, then a voice begins to chant. Alone, clear, triumphant, it sings the power of the God of Resurrections. The man rises, he has understood it all, he sets out again on his way.

Here are other ruins.

Are you partial to shrewd people? Do you like diplomacy in the affections? For my part I hate the last, and I am afraid of the former. This shrewdness, what is it but a little cunning employed in the service of much selfishness? If you love, you will have no cunning of the kind, nay you will have a certain awkwardness, and so much the better.

I am searching for men so thoroughly in love with an idea that they forget the interests of their own celebrity ; for combatants who storm the breach regardless of blows ; persons who can trample without a scruple upon their own glory ; crush their respectability ; are content to think differently from others ; who carry their convictions high, who bristle with principles ; awkward, if you like ; who present you with their creed just as it is, without dressing it up to please you, and positively I do not know where to find them ! There may perhaps be two, or even three such ; yes, I think there are ; people call them firebrands, and keep them at arm's length. To make one's-self *possible !* that one would say was the great aim of our age ; thence it results that men are sometimes admitted, but that ideas are left outside the door.

Our age is intellectual, capable ; it glides between opposite dangers, it is skilful in tacking ; from time to time, on condition that the whole world shall applaud, it allows itself some deed of prowess. But as for embracing an idea, grasping a theory, maintaining it with a high hand ; scorning all scorners ; consenting to contempt ; declaring that one is on the losing side ; for the minority against the majority ; that one is one's-self, and intends to continue so, and to be nothing besides ;

do not think of demanding this from our present time.

For my part, I grow indignant at meeting so much prudence, so little temerity. The reason may be that our youth are gone away, for young people have that noble indiscretion that I mourn. But have then the young of our day really got it? Do we see them attach themselves with all the passion of high souls to any losing cause, any cause which has parted with everything except honour? Are our young men indignant, impetuous; do we ever hear of their doing great and hopeless things, do they continue to love what they see fall? Rather is not the being thoroughly alive and flourishing the primary condition of their devotedness?

What would I not give to hear those bursts of generous nonsense which were wont to escape from us when we were twenty! We sacked Europe; we threw to the winds fortune, prospects, common sense; we were revolutionary, we were frantic. If events had taken all that frenzy at its word, there would have been some grievous surprises indeed. But at all events, however exaggerated, our sentiments were sincere. The heart had it all its way, the head was disregarded. Imagination spread her wings, we wanted to soar and we soared. I would rather be Phaeton falling through the sky, than a hackney coachman snug beneath an archway.

But who is there that betrays his convictions?

Oh, no one! only, in order not to have to disown them, one takes care to have none. Or if some one conviction lingers still, hidden in the depths of the conscience, one modifies, weighs, dilutes it, till even those who hold an opposite opinion may find ours very tolerable. Has there not been invented, by way of designating these attenuated beliefs, an expression equally revealing and ridiculous,—the *good taste* of our faith? People have convictions which are in good taste; these may be worn, but faith by itself is out of date. There are only a few old-fashioned people who still venture upon positive colours; very bad taste that; we have invented neutral shades, neither red, nor blue, nor white, nor black, I defy you to define their hue exactly; and in this consists ultra refinement and distinction.

Tell me, for my part, of some great clown who walks straight on, of some dolt who breaks the windows in his way; some ignoramus who believes what he does believe; of a peasant of the Danube who knows how to love and knows how to hate; of one of these plebeian intellects which defend the undefended; one of those castaways who risk their skin in forlorn hopes. Find me some self-forgetting soul who dares to pronounce beautiful what Society has agreed to declare ugly; who links his sacred personality with the fate of an unpopular undertaking; who makes common cause with a compromised truth; who consents not to succeed, and follows his faith, even were it to the gallows-foot; only show me that man, I shall call him a hero.

When we are very young, we believe that every one has a heart; when no longer so young, we see that a good many people have no heart at all, and that they carry a compass in its place.

Some one near has impelled you into the thick of the conflict, his voice has excited you. While success attends your steps that voice persists. Strong, sonorous, it does more than sustain your courage, it calls forth your utmost powers. You conquer, all is well; depend upon that man. But fortune turns, and defeats occur. Your courage has not abated; truth has not changed; you will defend it to the last; defend it all alone if need be. But no! my other self is there, and mutilated as I may be his arms are open to me. Indifferent people may be amused at my reverses, the world may applaud my enemies, multitudes that had followed may desert our cause; all that, one foresees, and little heeds. *He* remains to me, and that is enough. As soon as I have pressed him to my heart, my strength, my faith, my hope will all return. But what is this? A formal figure greets me, a stiff manner keeps me at a distance ; something frozen comes between us. It is he no longer : can it be I? I was wrong, he tells me, to throw myself into the battle. When one is badly armed, weak, and ignorant of warlike tactics, he should not attempt to fight. I have compromised truth it seems. And again, this truth, is it so certainly true? A stupefaction comes over me, a disgust, a nausea. Better the sword of the adversary than this reed which breaking pierces me.

You put forth some work ; a poem, a picture, a piece of music. Discreet people are silent, they wait. The bolder spirits at once declare themselves for or against. At all events those who do not consult the current of popular opinion will retain their own. Not so. You are praised, they clap hands ; you are attacked, their enthusiasm wavers. However exaggerated the blame may be, your friends find, looking more closely, that it has a substratum of truth. What they had approved, they see upon further consideration to be of little worth, and they tell you so frankly. To think differently from the rest of the world ! What, had you really expected that of them? Was it reasonable to do so? Just at first their partiality for you had misled them ; forgive them for it ; public good sense has set them right again. As for you who are down, they consider that it will do you good, and they leave you there.

This friend loved me in his sadness; he wanted me, I amused him, or some undertaking of his required my devotion ; others come who are both newer and more gifted, he melts away and escapes me. Another took pleasure in me when out of society; the neighbourhood of the great city detracts from my value ; our friendship is too rustic, too countrified ; the susceptibility of the more refined might take umbrage at it, and if he still gives me a portion of his heart, he at the same time apologizes for doing so to his indifferent acquaintances. A third is true to me so long as the sky remains blue ; so long as there is health and cheerfulness, and all things go smoothly in my home, I may depend upon him. When everything shakes, he vacillates ; when all gives way, he is swallowed out of my sight.

But, thank God ! however, if there are treacherous affections, if there are that are cowardly, if some break down and others fly away, there are also valiant tendernesses, there are hearts who know how to love. The earth might quake, the heavens melt, you would still find them true. They retain all their sympathies, their affection grows with your distress. They loved you when the favour of the world offered you its incense ; they love you still better now the world has deserted you. Your isolation, far from repelling, attracts them ; their fidelity is increased by the general defection ; your foibles can never weary them, nor your misfortunes detach. Sincere, yet at the same time partial, they tell you the truth, but they do not crush you with it. They have a mother's compassion to soothe your sorrows, they have a father's ambition to excite your courage. They would see you active, believing, generous ; your happiness is dear to them, your worth dearer still. Affections such as these, stronger than death, if God has given to you, oh, see that you guard them well !

I would fain stop, but I cannot do so. Always, there are devastations in my way.

Friends have failed me. Will our children answer to our hopes ? This son of mine will follow in my steps. He is a weapon of good proof, wrought with my own hands. His faith will be mine ; he will serve the cause that I have served ; the same ideas will make the hearts of both beat high as surely as the same blood throbs in the veins of both. We shall labour together before I die. His ardour will rekindle me, my experience will calm him ; and when I go, part of myself will be left behind.

And now see, here is your son, your favourite
son, the son for whom you have prayed so much,
loving you, for his part, very composedly indeed!
The emotions that agitate you leave him unmoved;
your beliefs are not his opinions. You thought
that he would walk by your side along the same
road, and that your arm, which had so long protected him, would henceforth lean upon his youthful and vigorous arm. Not so; your son has taken
another path; he is rapidly leaving you. Your
ways lie in different directions; what you respect
he sneers at; he avows what you disapprove; his
silence, and the few words that escape him, alike
attest his opposition. A silent, slow process of
alienation is going on; first in thought, then in
feeling, then in everything whatever. And in your
heart there echoes that cry that comes down from
age to age: 'Oh my son, Absalom! Absalom! my
son, my son!'

But even this is nothing. If vice have not
withered the soul of your child, you may still thank
God. The one real, one intolerable destruction,
look you, is not that which separates, but that
which corrupts; never resign yourself to the last.
Better a son who is the enemy of your ideas, than
one who is the enemy of his own soul. Let him
escape from your influence, but not from the pity
of his Heavenly Father. Lose him, if so it must

be, but oh, let him not be lost! The destroyer may do what he will; if you continue instant in prayer, still you shall snatch his prey from him. You may, indeed, have to bear it away torn and bleeding; but he will not have power to prevent its being all your own.

Beaten by contrary winds, stripped of all that disappointment can take from us, thus we arrive at length into the shady regions of mortal life. Some among us reach these early; some are long before they do so, but almost all descend hither at the last. We pass through these regions as strangers, with rapid and furtive step, like exiles hastening to some other land. Here we are lighted only by reflection; here the ear is no longer pleased except by faint echoes; we are warmed by happiness that is not ours. Like travellers we draw near to the hearths of others; the rays glide off from us to light up youthful faces; joys go and blossom in new and warmer hearts. We become isolated; scarcely does the place that knew us know us now; it is but our shadow, one would say, that returns to wander there.

We are no longer necessary to any one; the existence of those whom we love best will easily accommodate itself to our disappearance; the world has left us; the sounds of life die out; the current

has passed us by, bearing onward barks all laden
with a new generation. A harmony fills the air;
clapping of hands, shouts, laughter, songs! then
all is gone.

Stranded, we remain where the last tide left us.
The sympathies and antipathies of the world have
ceased to agitate us; those who felt them live no
longer. When some belated one hurrying on to
join the rest meets us, he is astounded; he had
believed us dead. Human life, the sun of mankind,
the earth's poetry, all these are opening out elsewhere, and if our trembling hand try to retain the
cup, the impatience of the living snatches it away.

Alone of all our race? Yes, we actually are so;
strangers to ourselves and to others. Our sorrows
fall back heavy on our own hearts; some may pity
them out of kindness, no one shares them. Formerly when we wept, eyes now closed grew wet
with tears; there were silent interrogations which
relieved us from the silence of sorrow; our smile
used to bestow happiness. Now nothing moves.
Snow lies on the face of all the land, so flowery
and so fragrant of old; an absolute silence prevails there.

Have you ever penetrated into the realm of
everlasting frost; have your steps sunk a whole
day through in the monotonous whiteness of the
snow-fields; has the solemnity of those solitudes

ever weighed upon your soul; has the pallor of those lonely summits, the majesty of those lifeless expanses beneath their winding-sheet, occasioned you a sadness as immense as themselves; have you seen the wings of the benumbed butterfly vibrate for the last time upon a ground all sparkling with frost; and have you found yourself passionately desiring the verdure of meadows and the songs and stir of the woods; has the cold of evening seized you, the light gone out, the shadows come down? You know then what it is I mean.

In like manner our happiness departs; life's currents have borne it away. They have borne away too a portion of ourselves. Ideal charms, good graces, ardour, all these;—where are they now? Alas! no one cares about them; no one thinks of asking them from us. If any one would seek, he might perhaps find them still; but no, people view us as dull, as worn out, and they are content to leave us alone.

I assure you that beautiful illusions do good; they expand the heart that retains, they fertilize the heart that inspires them. We do really possess the qualities others attribute to us. Whatever you expect from my affection, or desire from my intellect, I have; your hope has given it me. And do not suppose that such illusions deceive. Like the hazel wand, they guess at springs that have not yet flowed; like those miraculous rays of the old legend, they penetrate the soil, and kindle the iris of precious stones buried in the earth. So soon as no one expects anything from me, no one requires anything, I no longer have anything to give. The moment I am looked upon as dead, I am so. Motionless, I shall be less in the way. No one will come into contact with me except on the material side; I shall no longer render any sound but that of dry bones. I was alive, and if they had but chosen I might have been so still; but as it is, I am conscious of falling to decay. They have pushed me off the scene where the interests of the world are being transacted, and they have done right. My faculties desert me; my will alone— oh misery! survives in this great shipwreck, tenacious in proportion to its impotence, puerile and over-excitable both. My memory, like a page of blotting-paper covered with diverse hand-writings, presents only grotesque figures and confused lines; a mist rises between me and my thoughts; the cords hang loose; I drag myself along, looking back the while; my face turned towards what was, towards what has ceased to be; what will be in the future no longer concerns me. Marble, stucco, bas-reliefs, statues, one after the other, detach themselves, fall, disappear, and the wave that covers them displays itself to the sun. The little children will come to wet their naked feet there ; the young girls will dip in their urns, laughing the while ; not one shaft of a column, not one mutilated carving, will testify of the splendour past.

Everything comes to an end. There are hours when from the whole earth one sob seems to rise. The sweet summer evenings, together with their hymns of joy, have their heart-breaking wail. It is as though nature wept her own decay. The moon casts a mournful lustre on the earth ; the wind of evening sighs as it passes through the leaves ; the lake sends forth a monotonous and melancholy note ; the light falling from the sky breaks upon its surface ; the shimmering of the water scatters and quenches it ; dark clouds move across heaven like funeral processions ; I know not what voice seems to spread through the country the prophetic cry : The end is at hand—the end draws near !

For many people, and for many things, the end is already come; gaps have been made ; hands have ceased to press ; voices will sound no more.

But must we pause here ? Are we made to bury ourselves like fossils beneath mountains of ice ? Did God create us for this ? Is our soul to annihilate itself in a despairing farewell ; are our whitened bones merely to mark on desert sands

the march of successive generations; is there
nothing beyond? Have we nothing to expect?
Has God promised us nothing?

I hold the clue to all destruction and decay; it
is eternal life.

Who is there who could quit without reluctance
an earth where things retained their pristine brightness? If it were to realize all its promises, why
should we look elsewhere? And if I myself am to
be always beloved; if, instead of losing aught,
I march on from acquisition to acquisition, what
shall I ask from heaven? You tell me that God
has prepared it for me, that he has prepared me
for those ethereal dwellings? This earth is beautiful, good, and familiar; leave me here.

Ah yes, I remain here altogether. I aspire to
nothing higher; I mould myself upon inferior
types; I bring myself down to what I have; my
soul, which fears to lose its footing, skims the
ground. What is that country on high? Do not
speak to me of it; I am contented with that which
is below. To live in a purer atmosphere? Wherefore, when I breathe so comfortably here? To
meet my beloved ones for ever!—but here they
are; I hear them, touch them! To know Jesus!—
I have already met him. To take possession of a
glorious body!—mine serves and suits me well
To act in the plenitude of powers fully grown!—my
intellect has not failed me, my faculties have not

grown rusty. To triumph over ruin and decay; to rise revived, strong, young with that youth that God bestows !—why, in truth I am not conscious of being in any way ruined, nor old, nor even weak. Go, carry your heaven to others! Our own earth, cracked as she may be, satisfies me.

Do you see my drift? As for me, I imagine that if the people of Israel had not for forty years wandered in the Wilderness, they would have cared but little for the promised land.

Yet I know well, believe me, that God is not obliged to consume us to awaken in us the thirst for heaven; this may be equally born in happiness. The joys of a loving soul will never prevent it from adoring the Saviour. Happy though it may be, the sadness of sin will make it sigh for deliverance. It will seek its God amidst the delights of Eden, as it follows after him through the desolations of an accursed world. I have seen lives full of hope; I have seen flowers, yet humid with morning dew, transplanted into the celestial regions; have seen the serenity of joy ineffable lighten up brows that had not one furrow.

But, once more I repeat, I am writing for the sad, for the defeated, for the bereaved.

To those whom the Lord is leading through the rocky plains of Sinai, he points out the gushing fountains, and the waving trees, and the fresh hills, of Canaan.

V.

SOUL-TORTURE.

DOUBT is much in vogue at the present time ; very agreeable dissertations respecting it are put forth; it is an exercise which allows the many-sidedness of the intellect full play ; and certain individualities would even consent thus to oscillate on, in a wave now luminous and now dark, without ever coming to a stand-still. In this wave are found sundry effects which are fantastical indeed, but yet attractive. The very indecision of the forms assists imagination, without enslaving it, and, moreover, doubt looks well.

To take a decided part ! It is only roughly constructed minds that can consent to this. You must have inferior souls made by machinery, so to speak, to believe what they believe, simply, sincerely—let us speak out—sillily. He that believes, furnishes you with a scale by which to measure him; he who doubts, gains greatness by all the indefiniteness of his scepticism. If there are mysteries in faith, there are certainly many more in incertitude; for after all, through faith, I touch and I possess; while, on the contrary, so long as I remain undecided, the objects of my examination, even down to my own thoughts, all efface themselves as I draw near, and incommensurable horizons ever retreat before the doubting soul.

Ah! let us leave scholastic dissertations alone; they have no place here. You have doubted, I have doubted, and doubt is hell in the soul. While we doubted, despair seized hold of us, the abyss had swallowed up its prey; we rolled in the void; there was not a spot on earth to turn to,— not one place of refuge in the heart; everything was against us, because nothing could save us from the dissolution of our whole being.

There are doubts that traverse the soul like a lightning flash. They touch this or that point, smoke escapes, something has taken fire and been consumed; but for all that, the soul is not dead; although ravaged, the vital principle is there still. But when doubt slowly mounts like the vapours exhaled by swamps; when it hovers with pestilence beneath its wings, dissolves the very fibre of belief, fuses the energies, puts a feverish tremor and a morbid disgust in the place of the equable and healthy aspirations of life, why, then it is indeed the last agony and indeed death.

As for me, I cannot possibly play with it. Doubt, when it comes upon me, does not advance with the graces of a fencing-master ; it is a duellist in dire earnest. It is worse : it is one of those barbarians escaped from the olden time ; one of those brutal forces, let loose in its ignorant ferocity. With club in one hand and torch in the other, it falls upon everything that it sees; an insatiable appetite of destruction urges it on ; it neither selects nor spares ; it simply breaks down whatever comes in its path,—that is the shortest way. Then, standing on the ruins it has made, it looks round and marvels at the great silence that prevails. •

Other minds stop midway; others have lame doubts,—a timid scepticism ; they deny just so far, and no further; certain truths are sacrificed beforehand, the convenient appellation of secondary truths having been invented on purpose for them. For fear the devil should play his part on too great a scale, some are content to play it for him. Or it may be that their soul, better guarded, only admits fragmentary doubts. It is not so, however, in our case ; questions suggest them-

selves in all directions; they are audacious, have
no polite scruples, are restrained by no pity.   In
vain may you seek, like the Swiss hero, to concen-
trate all their spears upon your own breast; they
will pierce you indeed, but they will still stride on.

If, after all, there were no God! If the universe
had come of itself out of nothingness into being,
to return to nothingness again ! If I were only
leading my semblance of a life amidst the sem-
blances of other lives ! If this were to last as long
as last the ephemera of an autumn day; if afterwards I were to lose myself in a night peopled by
other phantoms alike deprived of existence, alike
the sport of I know not what fluctuations ; if blind
forces impelled by chance controlled the course of
the world ; if the heavens were empty ; if prayer
were useless ; if Jesus were not come ; if the Word
of God were a lie !

Have you felt the deathly chill ? Satan has
placed his hand upon my heart.   He reminds me,
speaking in a low and gentle voice, of that sufferer
whom Jesus did not heal ; shows me that son for
whom I pray, and who goes on wandering ; points
to my incapacity that God leaves great as ever,
my wants that he has not satisfied, my sin that
he has not subdued, even my doubt which dares
to rise up against him !   Once Christ was wont to
raise the dead ; once the Holy Spirit did convert

souls ; once God was known to work miracles ! Now !— Satan goes no further. He is not extreme; he will not take advantage of the power of logic ; he leaves it to me to draw the necessary inferences.

You have experienced this in the great crises of life. These thoughts have haunted you during the fatal night when the existence of some beloved being was slipping away from your grasp. ˙ When the earth shook, yawned ; when all your happiness was about to be swallowed up, you saw—did you not ?—the stars of heaven disappear ; and when the past no longer existed, and the present hour tortured your heart, you felt the future, too, crumbling away. You know what it is at those terrible moments to seek for God—shall I dare to say it —for any god whatever ; and to find none. You have pursued after him with vehement prayers, and those prayers have fallen back dead about you, like arrows shot into the air. Or else you have struggled in deep depression beneath the burden of the vanity of all things, and your cry for help has been lost without the most distant echo even to show you that somewhere it had been heard.

There are worse shocks still ; the apparent instability of truth,—the truth for which we suffer, for which we bleed. I believe myself to be standing up for the truth ; that it is indeed God and his

cause that I am serving; and all my confidence
and courage comes from this belief. Suddenly
truth vacillates; they tell us that God is angry,
that our boldness offends him, that we are in
error, that we war against God. Lost to me
beneath anathemas, oh where, my God, shall I find
thee now? Truth, how shall I recognise thee?
Who shall assure me that my conviction is not
pride? Who shall prove to me that my faith-
fulness is not revolt?

Tell me, do you find that this torture of the
soul is endurable? Can you smile at it; can you
discuss it? Alas! I am only a very simple creature, but this is what I do in such a case. I throw
myself on my knees, and I ask for faith. You
shrug your shoulders! Then tell me where I shall
find light, for light I absolutely must have. My
fellow-men cannot give it me, superior though they
be; the infinite is veiled from them as much as
from me. They may indeed lead me far on in
the paths of reasoning, but reasoning is not
light; they may conduct me to the ultimate point
their own wisdom has reached—that point is not
the sun. Men deceive themselves; things deceive
me; to address myself to my own mind is to turn
in a vicious circle. I go straight to God. If need
be, I will even repeat the very absurd and yet very
sensible prayer, bold, and yet full of holy humility,

of a doubting soul in its distress,—My God! If there be a God!

Who else than God, indeed, could enable me to find God? And so soon as I know that there is a God, who but he should take pity upon me? My God, come to me in this way of despair where I am; lift up thy prostrate creature from the earth. Believing myself to adore thee, I am perhaps all the while adoring some monstrous idol; oh, break the idol, were it to entail the breaking of my heart! If the truth I am holding so fast be an error, tear away the error, even though thou tear my vitals with it. My God, save me from myself; defend me! Here will I remain, prone, till thou answerest me. To-morrow, I will begin again, and the next day, and every day. It is not possible that thou shouldst, without heeding it, see thy child die.

But our heart is not only an alembic where ideas are elaborated; it is a volcano, throwing out its lava. I do not think any earnest man can look down into this crater without a shudder.

There are people who do really and in truth believe themselves good. This opinion might, indeed, have its sweetness; only, in order to retain it, it is necessary never to have met with one's-self. I mean with one's true self. Look then, here it

K

is, that terrible and ridiculous Self; that despot with vast ambition and paltry claims; that destroyer of my happiness; that eternal enemy of my soul. A hideous selfishness sometimes swells and invades my being; sometimes it contracts; becomes slippery, sinuous, and wraps me in its coils. Wherever I go, I meet with it; I detest, yet cannot shake it off. When I think I have fairly driven it away, it returns like a subtle odour, and vitiates the very air I breathe.

Take the most humble souls amongst us; the most at leisure from themselves; yet self is not dead within them. I grant you indeed that they do not flatter, but they are occupied with it for all that. This self will allow you to study, to criticise, even to revile it; so long as it may retain its place, even were it on the pillory, it will remain satisfied. Read the correspondence of men of mark; go and surprise their thoughts in those private journals that publicity yields up to us; the secret, the divinity, the monster crouching in the recesses of the holy of holies, is still their own self. Some carry it on high in full light, displayed upon their banners; others, who have the modesty of good taste, conceal it beneath the folds of the flag; but just let a puff of wind come, and the standard, as it unrolls, will show the sacred insignia.

There are consciences. I am well aware, who do

contend with this indefatigable wrestler; they keep their footing; nay, they even gain ground, they punish him, throw him; but, chained though he be, very often out of the depths of his prison it is egotism that reigns and governs still. We prefer to hate self rather than to forget it. Why, look you now; when I meet a man who does not contemplate himself, does not care about himself; a patriot whose passionate love of his country frees him from all anxiety about the part he plays; a philosopher whom the pursuit of a theory exiles from self-love; a poor uncultivated mind but yet indifferent to personal cares; an individual of any kind, in short, who is neither his own first nor last love,—I feel refreshed as by the aspect of a fountain of living water.

Selfishness! why, it will not grant me a single moment's respite. I speak; it listens to me; it dictates this word, and keeps back the other. I walk; it dogs my footsteps; like that double that the Germans see on their Hartz mountains, it reflects me, and constantly shows me my magnified image. If I weep with those who weep, it points me out my own tears; if I stretch out my hands to the poor, it makes my alms ring abroad; if I sing, it praises my voice; if I laugh, my gaiety. By a supreme effort I escape from it, and assert my simple self: oh, what nature, what independence!

I grow angry, I command it to be silent! at once it transforms itself. 'Yes,' it will now say, 'you are right, you *are* vain, unpleasing, foolish, hideous.' Me ; always me ; oh, who will deliver me from myself !

Fastened up tight by a short chain, we turn and turn round our pivot ; the soil we tread, beaten hard by our footsteps, ceases to be fertile ; our heart grows hard, our brain dry ; an inevitable impoverishment attends all who feed upon self.

And see, at this very moment that I am fighting hand to hand with egotism, the sterilizing breath has passed over me ; a void prevails ; air fails me.

I have met with it in my best affections.

It glides in surreptitiously between me and those I love, so that when I believe myself to be pressing them in my arms it is it that I really clasp. It mows down their joys, and puts my convenience in their place ; it insinuates itself into my emotions, and when they would overflow, dries them up. I would not count and calculate, but it does. It permits me to give, but forbids me to give myself. It renders me hard, nay cruel. A few moments of chat would enliven my aged father— Perhaps so—but then the arrangement of the whole day would be disturbed. A moment lost, and the whole is over !

If I were to remain this evening alone with my wife. Remain, only then thou must remain to-morrow, the day after,—every evening in short; goodbye to thy liberty.

If I were to marry off my daughter. Marry her! old as you are, without friends, without relatives, and then live all alone afterwards, be thy own vis-a-vis; sick and overlooked, thou wilt soon discover what it costs to be so vastly generous. Besides, thy daughter is happy; all the world is happy with the exception of thyself; look at home!

Do you remember those Mexican idols that used on days of high festival to be smeared over with human blood?

The priest, without swooning with horror, was in the habit of rubbing their faces with hearts that still beat. The idol lives, I tell you; it is seated in the deepest recesses of our soul, and if we look close we see blood upon it.

To live for self, to take care of self, to love self only in those one loves; to find self even in one's self-surrender to God; to confess that one prefers self to all besides, however hateful one may see this self to be; to consent to this, to grow accustomed to it—this is hell!

It seems as though I were wandering in those valleys of desolation where eternal frosts block up every way of egress; the eye seeks to escape in vain. At each exit a cold, stiff, inaccessible pyramid rears its impassable barrier.

What is it that dries the eyes of the orphan? What disputes with the workman about the price of his toil, takes his work, and cuts off a morsel of his bread?—Selfishness!

Selfishness has its religion; for itself, of course; it will be found ready enough to insure its own salvation; but that of others—never! I have got out of danger, let them get out as they can. Die, weep, be hungry, thirsty; selfishness, provided only you do not inconvenience it by your groans, it will leave you alone; it has no nerves.

Neither has it any distractions; I defy you to surprise it in a fit of absence; and as it is always at home, so is it a complete despot; and when a flood of love rushes over your heart, when some charitable impetuosity is about to sweep you away, it will know how to say, in its curt and imperious tones, ' Thus far and no further.'

We have all felt on our shoulders that horrible creature of the *Arabian Nights*—the little old man of the sea. Yes, it is he indeed; spiteful and tenacious; he has sprung upon his prey from behind, has stuck his claws into my flesh. He was puny, he is become strong; he was humble, he commands now; he holds on tight, he urges with his heel; my vigour passes into his veins, he sucks my heart's blood; heavy, and ever more heavy, I cannot shake him off; it is in vain that I dash myself in despair upon the ground; in vain that I bruise, crush him; he still clings fast, he will cling till the hand of my God tears him away.

And it shall tear him; God has promised this. We, who refuse to submit to so vile an outrage—we, who will never consent to the degradation of serving such a master, let us cease to lament, there is something of submission in these very tears. Let us trample upon selfishness, crush it; let us love widely, strongly; let us remove our centre, carry our glances further, higher, breathe a fresh air that will restore our life!

But see, here we have this repudiated selfishness taking an honourable name; it calls itself ambition, a noble ambition. To shut the door against it,— as well enter a monastery at once! Why, chosen souls adopt it in the face of the universe: they tell us that they owe to it their highest developments. And what, pray, would become of society if you took away the ambitious out of its system? Let us then receive the divine guest! The thing is done, here it is firmly settled within us.

What! this is its first word; what, you are vegetating in the shade! What! no one knows you! you contract your wishes to merely giving some paltry

little pleasure to some little commonplace people.
What! you have neither an official character, nor
a situation, nor anything that distinguishes you
from the general run of men? What! not one
prominent feature in thy whole existence? What!
thou wilt die, and, with the exception of thy wife
and children, and some poor people, obscure as
thyself, no one will ever remark thy death! Thy
name has never figured in the columns of a newspaper! This neighbour, that relative, who were
by no means thy superiors, take rank in the dis-
trict; they have weight, they are looked up to;
and thou, what art thou, then? A Christian, a
citizen, a parent,—is that anything to speak of?

To be something! Once let that idea get
rooted in the heart, the heart has its tyrant.

Do not misapprehend me. I can well understand the passionate love of action. Am I one
who would limit the range of the human mind?
Whoever feels himself strong, will exercise his
strength; this is the legitimate right, nay, the duty
of life; and I see no fairer spectacle, I scarcely
know any grander teaching than a life consecrated
to the pursuit of truth. When man can get out of
self to follow the fortunes of an idea; when he
falls in love with a cause, fights for some public
question, compromises himself, forfeits life, if need
be, for the honour of his conviction,—why, that is

glorious, the general level is raised, and the whole world receives an impetus forward. We are not, then, treating of the lovers of an idea, but of the lovers of their own selves. We may know these by their sadness. Mortifications meet them on every side. Now, the ideal exercises none of those cruelties toward those who serve it. These are the stigmata of human idolatry, which requires its martyrs, and marks them with wounds.

A fever has been kindled within me. Do not come to discourse to me of family sorrows, or obscure family joys, or of the pleasure that I give to this dear one, or of the affection felt for me by that dependant. To what purpose to me are such glow-worm sparks as these? What I want is to shine, and that it should be generally known that I exist, and that I should be talked of, and taken note of. My emotions, you see, and my happiness come from notoriety. Am I really known; has my name been seen printed at full length in a newspaper; are my talents, my distinctions, nay, were it only my money, noised abroad? If some one were to run to me with that intelligence, welcome indeed be that friend; he brings me sunshine. To play a prominent part on the world's stage, I feel capable of all sacrifices whatever; I will take interest in the Turks, the Greeks, the Chinese; I will become a philanthropist, espouse public affairs; my fortune, my family, my time, myself—take them all; but give me shouts, give me the trumpet-blast for my portion, and, down to the very grocer in the corner of the street, let the whole republic know that I am somebody.

You laugh at this caricature; for me, I find the original in my own worthless heart! Ah! when I want to know whether it is myself that I idolize or truth that I love, I look upon the success of my companions in arms, and if my soul triumphs in their victories; if, when a mind more highly endowed than mine defends our mutual faith better, my whole being exults; if, when another intellect, inferior perhaps, succeeds in making acceptable what I failed to get understood, I feel a true delight; if that man realizes the good I would fain have accomplished, if he reaps where I sowed, if, in the triumph of our common cause, he is celebrated and I am forgotten, and I the while can raise both hands sincerely, and exclaim, I thank thee, O my God!—yes, then mine is indeed a noble ambition, the ambition of angels. But if silence distresses me; if obscurity stifles; if the successes of others freeze up my ardour; if my heart contracts at the praise given to them; if I would rather see the cause I believe in dead in my hands, than thriving in my neighbours, why then I am an egotist; I suffer the tortures of an egotist; my wound may

seek in vain to disguise itself beneath royal vestments,—it is the wound of egotism.

I will tell you the horrors of a sadness of this
kind; it cannot dwell with God. As a slave, as a
victim of the world's misapprehensions or my own
errors, weary, ruined, it mattered not, still I could
go and find my God; he lived within my sick
heart; but as a confirmed egotist, I cannot do so;
so long as I am my own god, how should I possess
God? There is something of Satan the accursed
in that which struggles and rages within me.

Mortified, mortifying, hard to those who love
me, devoured by this barren pain, a prey to the
delirium of pride, unsocial, ashamed of my suffering,—so I drag on. Do you remember the story
of the Venus of Illo? do you recall that impassive
embrace of the bronze statue? I tried to seize the
idol; its arms have closed around me. Unless
some mighty stroke break its limbs, I die; its
cruel smile accompanies my agony. All idols
have this same infernal malice.

One step further into the darkness.

I am conscious of a hostility, almost a hatred,
taking possession of my heart.

Oh the good that a perfect love does us all!
How fain would I lose myself in one of those
affections where we are incessantly giving, caring

little to know whether we are receiving in return; yes, it is so I would love; I would believe everything, hope everything, endure everything. The soul is made for these intense attachments, as the bird for the vast plains of the air. And now, behold a sentiment of repulsion is stirring within me. I have been made to suffer; I fear and I hate.

The defects of a certain nature irritate me; its very virtues put me out of patience; so distasteful, indeed, are they, that I am not sure but that I should prefer imperfections that were more congenial.

This man compromises my future, exerts an inimical influence around me. How then can I think well of him? Then the next step is that I think ill, nourish myself with gall; commend my own irritation; the demons that were sleeping within me wake; they smite me with their serpents; at each sting I feel a kind of excitement. Should any one come to tell me: That man is ill, I should not rejoice; that he was in pain, this would give me no kind of pleasure; but if I am told that he is wicked, if some unworthy action of his is related, then I am conscious of a diabolical satisfaction. Horrible, this! it is like dogs fastening greedily on carrion. And more! I nurse my antipathy. I do not want to love that man.

I might possibly consent to pray for him, but not to detest him less. Kill him! no, certainly; only do not let him stand in my way. And if, to remove him out of it, it be absolutely necessary that God should take him out of life,—well, be it so, let him go to another world.

Yes, there are murderous thoughts, silent and swift of flight as the bats that flit round us at nightfall; their cold wing has touched my brow.

I have a still more lamentable confession to make. I not only hate, but I am envious as well. Do not contradict me, my conscience cries out that it is too true.

One does not own such things, you say; one does not expose one's sores. And I, for my part, assure you, that the more we conceal them, the more they spread.

The happiness of others, when I was myself unhappy, has saddened me still more. When I have seen one who was rich, kind-hearted, generous, popular, celebrated, a question has risen to trouble my soul : Why should he be so, and not I ? This woman is beautiful, and for no other reason she displeases me. That intellect radiates, scatters happy sayings, has just views, all the world is conscious of its fascinations ; as for me, I remain apart ; that sound of delighted laughter makes me inclined to weep ; I wait till something foolish escapes the phœnix, to be pleased in my turn. That voice is sympathetic, has touching vibrations, its tone answers to the depths of the heart ; it is listened to with enchantment, I do not share that enchantment, I resist it ; those magnificent accents jar me ; I wait for a false note to applaud. Why should I be one of God's disinherited children ? Others possess talents which he has refused to me ; others exercise a charm,—as for me I have charmed no one. There are women whose every silly smile subjugates and bewitches ; I know not how to smile thus. That man speaks mere commonplaces in high-sounding language, everybody bows ; his commonplaces are approved, he is the fashion, his place is ready made for him ; and I, who am better worth by far, I am not listened to, I am not looked up to, I cannot establish my own poor little footing in the sunshine. See those eyes beaming with mirth, and that brilliant complexion, and that gay laugh ; to her, smooth, easy days are allotted. I too, my eyes might beam as brightly, if God chose ; my face would be fresh too ; I am young as she is ; I might welcome every morning as it came ; but no ; God has bowed me down ; laden my soul with gnawing cares ; filled my life with insupportable suffering. When that woman passes me, when the air, perfumed by her happiness, reaches me, it is as though I had inhaled poison. My disease—an appalling one—is composed of the felicity of others ; my hideous enjoyments are made up of their griefs. I will console sufferers as much as you like ; I will go as often as you will into the house of mourning ; only, do not take me to the happy ; do not oblige me to enter homes that abound in all the blessings of this life ; they stifle me. An ulcer is devouring my heart, how can you expect that heart to beat ? My eye—the eye of a night-bird—detests the light ; how would you have me look at the sun ? To admire ! I ?—I to dilate at the glories of moral beauty ; I to thank God for the gifts he has given to other men ; I to rise by comprehension ; to possess by sympathy ; to share the happiness sown all around,—that is what I cannot do. I am impoverished by the wealth of others ; the praise given to them humbles me ; the love felt for them withers me up ; all that they have is so much that has been stolen from me.

Thus our soul degrades itself. When I contemplate its depths, I see vices wheeling round there like vultures in an abyss. Sometimes a disgust of myself, a horror of my situation, a vehement desire to emerge into the divine light, have caused me to heave one of those great sighs, to make one of those mighty efforts which should reach the throne of God ; but there has been no response ! I have fallen back again, have sunk deeper. Let him who has made my soul be concerned for it ; for my part, I look at it with dry eyes, I can no longer weep.

You tell me to divert myself; I know what diversion is worth. Sometimes I make believe to be intoxicated thereby ; but I measure its inanity, and despise it.

If, at least, some terror would come to rouse me ! But no, I have the stupid consciousness of my own abject state, and yet not a fibre shudders. I think I may even come to make fun of my own tortures ; then will be heard that harsh laughter which responds to the anguish of the soul. Some winter night, by the dull glare of a street lamp, beneath snowy gusts, will be seen, in some low street, hanging to a bit of rope, the corpse of the man who laughed thus. Oh, how mournful it is when memory returns to these fatal images ; how well one can enter into those frenzies of despair ; how one yearns to cry out to the one who died thus, to cry through space and time : Stop! above the depths there is heaven ; above sin there is the Saviour !

But in the intoxication of grief, I go on to utter rebellion : I contend with my Maker !

God is not just, God has neither pity nor tenderness; and from this moment I have no longer any desire to turn to him; I shall not bend, shall not complain; my heart grows hard as flint; break it if thou wilt; ground down to powder, it will resist thee still!

And besides, what does God care about my perishing? It is all one to him. A little happiness would have restored me to him; some one poor joy in my life, and I should have prayed to him, adored him. Grief is unhealthy; he loads me with grief. Happiness would save me; he refuses me happiness. Immutable in the serenity of his heaven, he takes no heed of a creature like me. A word from him would give life to my child, strength to my husband, success to this or that enterprise. What is it that we ask? Only bread —only some fragments of that wellbeing of the soul that God showers on so many others. But it is all in vain; God does not listen to us. By what right does he afflict us thus? Becomes it then the King of heaven to persist in crushing the poor in the dust? Does that serve to increase his glory? If he thinks to regenerate me by these means, he is deceived; the excess of misery only rouses my indignation; bitterness floods my soul; each new grief sinks me lower still.

There are souls born meek; passive submission

belongs to their temperament ; it would cost them more to resist than to consent ; there are others proud, passionate, ardent, who can only endure what they willingly accept. Suffering occasions them an amazement which borders upon rebellion ; they feel at its approach something of the indignation of a king's son upon whose purple a slave has laid his hand. Such souls as these, who retain nothing of their high origin but pride, deal with God as with an equal ; the sentiment of their own sinfulness never reaches them ; the necessity of being purified, even by fire and sword, angers them ; believing themselves to be quite sufficiently ready for the heaven they are to enter by right, they only see a cruel tyranny, where the humble recognise an indispensable probation. They have no need of a Saviour ; the agonies of Jesus, which teach them nothing, do not touch them either. If the Son of God knew pain and languor, it was because he chose to know them ; their own martyr-dom is none the less for that. Let God obey their imperious prayers, and then they may acknow-ledge in him some compassion ; so long as he remains deaf, their hearts remain closed against him.

We who believe in the divine tenderness, we know these straits ever narrower, ever darker, as they go on. We have passed through them ; the shuddering impatience of desolation has attacked us too.

We have watched beside the bed where groaned some cherished sufferer ; his complaints tore our very soul in twain. If God would send him a little sleep ; if but for one short hour God would say to pain : Relax thy hold ! God does not say so ; the lamentable wail sounds on, the fevered glance wanders round, the arms still toss, and we, our strength to endure exhausted, feel rebellion ferment within: If thou wouldest! If thou wouldest!

The messengers of Job arrive one after the other; the ruin of projects, the uprooting of habits, disasters, death, anathemas,—these are indeed the kings that Scripture speaks of as making ready for battle. Each shoots his arrow, each pierces us with his lance, our life oozes away. Was all this indeed essential? Could God not have dispensed then with our misery? Has he no other means of converting men? no other secret of winning human love ?

Thou crushest me ; I let myself be crushed. Thou treatest me like an inert thing ; be it so, I am inert. Strike ; there is no longer any resistance, but there is no longer a heart either. Thou art the master ; thou smitest thy slave ; it is thy right to do so ; perhaps there is some need that **the slave** be smitten. Only do not call **me** thy son, nor ask from me what a son may give, love, confidence, tears shed upon thy breast ; the slave weeps at the corner of the highway, and dies there.

This strikes you as horrible ; there is one thing still more so, and that is an open conflict with God.

God wills, and I do not will ; God says—Thou shalt give me back that child : No, I will not give it thee back.   Part with thy life-companion : No, I will not part with him.   And my child sickens, and I see my other self die !   Oh, if I could pray, consent ; if, holding the hand of my beloved, I could keep close behind him on his way ; by faith, by my love, by the eternal mercy, I might enter in with him, I might go where he goes !   He soars all glorious ; he escapes from me, parts from me, and I cannot hold him back ; and I will not surrender him, and God takes him from me.

Ah ! I know well that there are triumphs for those who submit.   I have felt them.   With a heart crushed, on the very borders of revolt, I have invoked the help of the Holy Spirit ; by his strength I have been able to whisper, ' Thy will be done.' Then peace and freedom have revisited me.   I took my flight—I too—towards the skies.   I had done with the tortures of this world.   A power was given me. All in tears as I was, my breast still heaving with sobs, a song of praise resounded within me. It was the song of the redeemed of the Lord.

Nothing of the kind now. The savage roar of a wild beast, rather; worn and weary as I am, it is my will alone, my will excited, exaggerated, uncontrolled, that holds out against God.

You think, perhaps, that it is only some supreme event that can provoke such a state as this; that these frenzies of rebellion are reserved only for the tragedies of life. You are wrong. The merest trifle can raise this whirlwind of pride in my heart. As soon as God says, Do this, Satan replies, I will not do it.

I am a worm, and the worm braves the thunderbolt. My conscience is thoroughly awake. I see my duty; nay, I perceive its every detail with a morbid preciseness. I have the common sense which believes in the chastisement of God. I have not the faith which makes his mercy present and his help actual. I remain disobedient. That God should not annihilate me at once, that is indeed the crowning miracle of his love. What! must Jesus, the King of glory, learn obedience by the things he suffered, and shall I pretend to be exempt from suffering? Show me the son that has not obeyed; show me the father that has not exacted obedience; show me the redeemed Christian whose heart has not bled?

And do you suppose that it is my heart alone that bleeds? The Father has not then a Father's bowels of mercies? If there were any other method of renewing us, would not God take that method? Has he any pleasure at all in our cries? Did Jesus suffer for no cause?

These truths flash out in the midst of the storm. I will not see them. A madness seizes me. I give myself up to my madness. And now I remain proud, and I am lost!

There is no longer any place for repentance; the inevitable weighs upon me. In the midst of creation's harmonies, I only hear the words : Too late! The past casts them at me like a wreck that the tide keeps constantly bringing back; the present repeats them in its lifeless tones; they fill the future.

My memories are all remorse. Those hours —dull while I possessed them—rise in the reflorescence of a new growth; they show me what they would fain have given me ; what they expected from me ; then they pale and fade away; and it is *too late !*

A figure rises out of oblivion : I have only to meet that long, disappointed look, only to see those pale lips that asked so little, and my heart contracts. He will return no more, he whose hope I deceived; death has indeed taken him. I might have made him happy; I doled him out the poorest enjoyments. I profited by his discretion to protect my own selfishness. Oh, how I would fain cover his frozen hands with my kisses! If I could but throw myself at his knees, and ask his pardon! —Too late!

That other, I did him injustice: he loved me; and because he did not realize all my dreams, I disdained his heart, I wounded him mortally.

I have made my mother weep. In return for all her love, I spoiled her life. Or if I did not rend her heart, yet, was I indeed the child of her expectations? What she came and looked for in me, did she really find?

There are certain words; there are expressions of countenance; there are secret, forgotten unkindnesses, which all at once resume a living, breathing actuality, and each of these says to us— Too late!

The irreparable possesses this magic freshness of colouring; the soul, reduced to contemplate what no longer exists, has these incomparable refinements of tenderness. One hour, but one hour only! We would buy it with our blood! No; never! Neither to-day, nor to-morrow, nor throughout eternity, wilt thou find again the one whom thou hast made suffer! Never more wilt thou be able to tell him that thou didst love him spite of all! He has borne away his sorrow; he will never see thy tears!

My sins cover me like a garment! I had not been aware before of their hideous aspect. Satan shows them me; he dissects me alive; and beneath the floods of incredulity with which he deluges my heart, one conviction remains, alone and ineradicable,—a conviction that he spares, nay, fosters; that of the irremediable.

What I have done, what I have left undone; my coldness towards God, my fervours for self; the time I have lost, the hours I have spent ill; my antipathies, the bitterness of my soul; my idle languors, the hypocrisy of my words; my rebellion, my scepticism—all are there. Throughout all ages nothing will be able to efface them!

I hate myself; God hates me; horror possesses me; but I am not touched. I go my way, the way to damnation or annihilation. If God had willed, it need not have been so with me. God is my enemy. I feel an infernal gratification in calling Him unjust; the demons have joys like this.

God my enemy! His eye is fixed upon me to spy; His hand stretched over me to punish. I am scared Earth is dark. What should souls such as I do with pleasures, with love, with all that charms and deceives ? I have lost my God. Happy they who suffer and pray! I, too, with God by my side, could brave disease and bear bereavement. If only I could weep ; if only I could drag myself into his presence ! But to suffer alone ; to see myself die and be alone ; to go alone to confront his wrath ; to wander alone upon the earth that he has made so sweet to other men. I, the only one, without a God, without a Comforter ; reduced to myself, wicked ; given up to the madness of my sins ; abandoned by him who came to seek the lost. This, this is indeed an insupportable wretchedness.

You talk to me of distractions : I have a soul, and it cannot be satisfied with lies. You tell me of penitence and penance : I have a heart, and it cannot be filled with vanities like these. I want my God.

Were I to die of it, I will brave his presence. How endure to live without God ? He may slay me, but, oh ! let me feel his breath. Heaven without him would be empty. Look you, it is himself that I want. I know this. All other loves, if his love were lacking, would only bring me a worse desolation. If you gave me genius, what could I make of genius far from my God ? If glories were to abound, of what use is glory unless I possess my God? Without him, the tedium of life oppresses me, and the fear of dying keeps me clinging desperately to life. Of what use to seek to rise? What can I find above me if I fail to find God? And as for sinking lower, I have known him too much to delight in degradation.

Yes, it is true I might, like Ophelia, let myself be swallowed up by the waters; I might sink utterly in the immensity of a boundless misery. I see her still; beautiful; her young face shaded by wild flowers; stretched out without a movement; the water, about to cover her, ripples and laughs around her; her stiffened body sinks gently; your eye follows it through the cold transparency; not a fold of her garment is disarranged; the smile remains on her lips. But I, I repudiate the thought of annihilation; there is no such thing. The delirium of grief does not convince me. My soul cannot die. I have told you so before; whether as friend or foe, redeemer or judge, I must meet with my God!

I have met with myself, and that is the very reason why I detest myself, the very reason why I so need God. My sin has driven me out of self; I seek a deliverer. Had I been better satisfied with my own soul, a stranger to the sufferings of the hell there, I might perhaps have been content to leave God in his heaven; any faith whatever

might have sufficed me ; now I cannot do this.
Shipwrecked as I am, it is not a rope thrown from
far, and floating at random on the waves, that can
save me ; I want a hand.

There is one !

God's heart exists; God's indifference has no
existence. My Saviour has walked upon this earth.
A poor man, blind, naked, lying in the dust, cried
to him once : Have mercy upon me ! This is all
I know to say. Ah ! better the sorrow that throws
me prostrate at the feet of Jesus, than the inflated
ease of pride that once deceived my heart. If,
to comprehend the cross of Jesus, the extremest
agonies must assail me : seize me, all desolations
and pangs !—sinner as I am, I want to know
myself; it does me good to find myself hideous ;
I will take my leprosy to the healer of lepers :
Have mercy upon me !

My whole being utters these words. The whole
creation, had it a voice, would utter them too.

Have mercy upon me ! It is the cry that shakes
the gates of heaven.

Have mercy upon me ! the prayer has not yet
shaped itself upon my lips ; the Father has heard
it, has answered it ; angels weep with joy ; Jesus
takes me into his arms.

I do not know why, but while wandering amidst

these woes, a landscape that I saw one stormy evening kept constantly recurring to my memory.

Currents of hot air were blowing along the ground ; we were driving rapidly on ; the horizon before us was becoming hid by dense clouds ; their iron shield spread over half the sky ; the sun seemed to pause upon its edge, shuddering, one would have said, at being swallowed up of darkness. All colours had grown dull ; not one of those purple-tinted mists that wander at evening, gave brightness to the view. A sinister glare, a strange light, clearer than belonged to the hour, struck here and there, on field or road. One heard no thunder, but in that prodigious mass of clouds there were sudden shiftings, and, as it were, thrills, that marked the path of the storm. It was grand ; it was still more gloomy ; even the very silence inspired a sudden terror. If the thunder had pealed, if the lightning had rent the clouds, one would have felt it a relief.

The singular feature, however, and that which has impressed the picture upon my mind, was a large opening in the very middle of the darkness. There the sky was seen glorious in the serenity of a wondrous sunset. Nothing could equal that limpid radiance. It had no rays, no golden sheaves, no crimson flames ; only the blue transfigured with light, stretched, deepened, peaceful, eternal ; it was all one saw. Meanwhile a mist began to rise from the darkened country. It rose wreathing, tending towards that clear sky. Its spirals now intertwining, now severing, re-formed, and always they rose.

Between those bewildered mists, so resolute to reach the sky, and the painful effort of the human heart, I detected one of those harmonies which give us the secret of our sorrows. Desolate souls rise thus ; one and the same movement, full of anguish, full of hope, bears up the phalanx of supplicants, bears them on to God.

And I, I found myself weeping **for joy.**

VI

BEAUTIFUL SADNESS.

ERE is a ridiculous title, indeed—
Beautiful Sadness. What, pray, may
this beautiful sadness be? Where
does this *rara avis* perch? who ever
took it into his head to combine two words so
utterly discordant?

In the time of Racine, indeed, one heard of the
beauty of tears; one heard too of the tears of
Aurora, the tears of the dew, and of the noble
despair by which beautiful souls were moved.
We, however, are realists, and give in to no such
nonsense. Tears by no means embellish; there
is no kind of charm in suffering; all unhappy
faces are ugly, all sadness displeasing. Happy he
who has never known sorrow, even though in
consequence he should never taste delight; and,
indeed, if you push us so far, we shall boldly

declare that it is the oysters who have drawn the first prize of existence.

Indeed ; you think so ?

People may vaunt the happiness of indifference, but who would have it ? Who would habitually press down the pedal that deadens all the tones of life ? Who would like to feel the regular oscillation of a pendulum, in lieu of the fitful beatings of the human heart ? Who, in the place of the infinite around, would build a wall, and knock up against it at every bound ?

Take my word for it, the saddest thing under the sky is a soul incapable of sadness.

He who has never experienced disappointment has never been enamoured of the ideal. He who thinks himself satisfied with earth has lost the memory of the skies. He who is neither tormented by a passion for truth, nor agitated by a desire for progress, walks in the low places of this world of ours, knows not that there are, high up yonder, peaks shining in the sun ; nay, scarcely knows whether there be any sun or not.

You point me out a character that is moderate, deliberate, neither sad nor gay, neither hopeful nor depressed ; one of those individualities which amble on, never pausing, never galloping, their head always on the level of the oat-bag ; and you tell me, Behold a wise man ! Not so. Wisdom—

the true wisdom—aims higher than this; returns to its source; placidity is.not its idea of happiness, any more than mediocrity is of existence. It would fain grasp all that God has destined for it, and consequently it aspires. It has the mighty impetus of the eagle sailing straightway to the light; it has the weariness of a pinion fatigued by distance and beaten by the tempest. It has the desire and the sorrows of the exile who looks constantly in the direction of his native land; and I prefer it thus, defeated and distressed, to those short-winded, short-sighted souls whose little tufts of wings are afraid of venturing upon space, and merely skim the highroad.

Yes, there are noble sorrows; there is a grandeur and a power in experiencing them. To regret, to desire; beneath these two sighs, horizons recede; by these two levers I can lift the world.

A man who neither regrets nor desires accomplishes nothing. He will eat and drink, will laugh perhaps, though indeed real mirth belongs to those who have felt real sadness. Those shrivelled-up characters whose narrow hearts are not capable of lodging so great a guest as sorrow, those rational people who submit to everything because incapable of resisting anything, have never excited my respect or my emulation. They remind me of barren . evergreens, all shrunk and withered beneath the heat of summer; a good shower would refresh and dilate them. Yes, but to have such a shower, one must consent to thunderstorms.

As for me, sadness, far from repelling, attracts me; I feel myself at home with her. Happiness enchants indeed, but it also amazes me. I feel as though I had met a celestial voyager; he is on the wing; I but touched, and I have lost him. Sadness is more faithful; she bent over my cradle; when I was a child she sang me her plaintive ditties; when young, she opened out her arms wide,—how often I have thrown myself into them! All my life long I have felt her beside me; if I try to take a step away from her, she beckons me back; if she leaves me for a while, I feel bewildered, almost alarmed, I know myself no longer. You do not accord her any charms, but she has beauties of a superior order. I call to witness that face, for instance; look at it; when merry it is vulgar; let sorrow come,—the expression of the eyes deepens, the lips find higher tones, a light transfigures the face, the divine impress breaks forth. We no longer have before us a race of Helots, content beneath blows, provided only they may satisfy their appetites; but a race enslaved, yet resisting, which will know how to shake off its yoke and regain its liberty.

Indeed, an immutable placidity might well be

M

supposed to conceal an immutable selfishness. If none are fit for the skies without having known a divine home-sickness, how can they be capable of divine love unless human affections have torn their hearts? Those to whom love has caused no suffering have never loved; all who have loved have wept. And this is a beautiful sadness. I give away my heart, it returns to me bruised; I do not regret it. Would I consent to love my son less, because my son proves ungrateful? If anything can bring him back, will it not be my very anguish and those intense prayers that are born from desolation?

That woman when she died carried away with her all my happiness; would I for that have loved her less?

My friend suffers; as long as his soul languishes mine is depressed. I will keep my depression; my sadness is precious to me; it is this which soothes him; a firm courage would intimidate, a more perfectly equable mood would close up his heart; bowed down both of us, prostrate at the feet of Jesus, our affection steeped in tears, leaves the cold serenities of philosophy far below.

Selfishness is all full of a species of resignation. For my part, there are woes for which I am resolved to know no consolation. I will never submit to live despoiled of beliefs. I will never grow accustomed to see without suffering the wounds of some poor broken heart. I will not consent to leave off loving ; I will not succeed in dispensing with the ideal. I will never buy repose at the cost of weakness ; the degradation of a precious soul shall not find me passive ; there are miseries by which I will be incessantly afflicted ; facts shall never be able to conquer me. At the bottom of some forms of happiness, I discover contempt of man and of God, and such happiness as this I positively refuse.

Ask yourselves, what would have become of us if Jesus had been resigned to see us wicked, to see us hardened, to see us lost ?

He who makes up his mind to a thing remains motionless, his heart grows introverted. He whom pain afflicts struggles against it. Suffering has left many conquered, but she has made many more conquerors.

Let us look at truth.

The desire for truth agrees ill with our comfort. When one values one's repose ; fears currents of air ; desires above all things to lead a quiet life, shaded from the sun, guarded from the rain ; pleasantly unfolding in the midst of general approbation, one is wise in leaving truth alone. Only truth does not always leave us alone. She fastens on certain minds, kindles them with the desire to possess her ; so soon as they have had a glimpse of her charms, they run after her ; precipices, quagmires, furnaces, nothing stops them, and this chase may go on long. You pity these people ! They do not pity themselves ; nay, they affirm this to be happiness.

But for all that, they are uneasy ; they satisfy themselves with difficulty ; they examine, prove ; a constant toil keeps them agitated. These men cannot put up with appearances ; a tolerable approximation will not do for them. Tell them not of salutary errors ; they smile sadly and pass on : do not try to convince them that what is false is useful ; they shake off your utilitarianism like a childish disguise. They are haunted by a pre-occupation very ridiculous and quite obsolete—that of principle. These singular beings, belonging, one would say, to some other planet, which has got jostled out of the universal order ; these fanatics, enamoured of the ideal, bitten with the mania of truth, run up into collision with consequences without even seeing them, and steer straight to the focus of light. As if there were a focus of light ! As if the highest reason did not consist in paddling as cleverly as possible through the diffused lights in which the world rotates !

Often have they been told that truth does not

exist; or that if there be a truth, it is in all cases
an impracticable creature, unmannerly, angular,
which goes blindly on like a cockchafer; that it
has a narrow intelligence, a cross temper, an obstinate will; that the best thing one could do in
the event of meeting it would be to turn one's
back at once; that people with proper self-respect
never involve themselves with such an unattractive
and discreditable character; that it compromises
a good reputation to be seen walking by its side;
but it is all in vain; these iron souls let you talk,
let you argue, and go on pursuing their chimera.

You think they are not aware of their malady?
They know and yet they cherish it. They are
infatuated to such a degree that your state of ease
has no attraction whatever for them. Nevertheless they suffer. The higher their aim, the oftener
it eludes them. One question solved brings to
light problems which are unsolved. Adieu to all
ready-made opinions; each conviction must. be
conquered in hand-to-hand fight.

You have read travellers' accounts of their fearful wanderings through primeval forests. Giant
creepers intertwine, thorns bristle; dead trees that
have fallen by accident encumber the ground; the
feet are bruised, the hands torn; sometimes a serpent
coiled round a branch darts out its wicked-looking
head; each step is a peril; every faculty is called

into play ; not a moment of relaxation ; it is a
struggle which requires the whole man. Yes ; but
they have also told you, have they not, the charm
of such a life ? They have described to you the
prodigious majesty of those solitudes ; that plenary
liberty; that sentiment of dominion ; that development of power; those glories of conquest; that consciousness of strength ; the enchantment of nature
seized and possessed in her pristine state ! Let
others glide along the river's flow, comfortably reclining, on the divans of some splendid steamer ;
let trains sweep them on beneath the dome of
forests where the rails have forced their way ; and
the journey over, let them find shelter in the apart-
ments of a palace ;—that is all very well. But we,
the true pilgrims, prefer the chance shot that gives
us our evening meal ; for us cold nights, with the
open sky and the stars above us, and the uprising
of the sun when his burst of glory makes the whole
earth shout for joy ! What would you have ? It is
so with the seekers after truth. Every morning
they set out afresh. A voice has said to them,—
Thou shalt go on for ever.

Not, though, that they are condemned to pursue
a mirage. What they have seen, they have
touched ; what they have touched they hold. But
they see beyond it. What, indeed, is heaven but
something that stretches out beyond !

The infinite which fills the soul and quenches its thirst, excites it in equal measure.

Why is it that an incomparable calm attends the study of the exact sciences? It is because they hardly raise any questions that they do not answer. The curiosity that they excite is sure to be satisfied one day. Their perspectives have much grandeur, but still they are definite; and stretch them out as you will, some age, some man will infallibly reach their limit. God, one might say, has allowed their chain with all its coils to lie upon the earth; and so soon as science has found one of its links, she is sure to lay her hand eventually on both ends; the mystery raised by one fact will be dispelled by another.

It is not so in the realm of abstract thought; one of the extremities of the ladder rests indeed upon the ground, the other reaches far beyond the starry immensities. This light bursts forth, you follow, you reach it; the dazzling path becomes a milky way; grows pale as it rises, and loses itself in the eternal depths.

Our faith gives us, indeed, that which our effort could never avail to grasp, but in order to maintain itself on the level of truth our faith must labour actively. No torpor for her, no relaxation; a combat without truce.

Consciences contented merely with **practicabi-**

lities ; souls fed at second-hand enjoy a sort of dull
placidity which does not warm them, but leaves
them quiet.   They do not feel much consciousness of life, they are seldom apprehensive of death.
They rise but little and sink little.   If they possess nothing, they have at least nothing to lose.
Men enamoured with the love of truth, those who
want to find God himself, take their flight now
through torrid and now through frozen zones; they
are like those pilgrims of the air who brave contrary
currents, and, while the earth is rejoicing in the
rays of the sun, struggle in the clouds against the
hail, blinded with snow, dazzled by lightning, their
breathing oppressed, and without a moment's
relaxation.   These men rise ; they do not stop
short ; the others remain crouching in regions
far below.

Nor are these their only sorrows. So soon as
a man serves truth, he must resign himself to displease.   Nor is it only the indifferent whom he
offends, he will pain friends besides !   That weak
people should find him absurd he could easily
bear ; but serious minds blame him, and this
troubles him.

He is proud, they say ; full of himself; intract-
able.   A terror seizes him.   Am I indeed such
a one ? and if I am, how can truth dwell with me ?

Once shaken, they shake him further; they ask him whether he supposes himself to be the only one right, and the whole world wrong; if he believes himself to be God's only confidant? They request him just to count those who walk by his side, and, above all, to consider what they are,—poor, ignorant, obscure; while the intelligent, the cultivated, camp in the ranks of the opposing army. Then burst forth within him storms that uproot oaks. He had believed truth to be firm, but it vacillates on its basis. His conscience had cried to him, Yes! thou art right; his conscience has now nothing but peradventures to offer. Not knowing to whom to appeal, his sight clouded too, his joints trembling, he falls down prostrate before his God. The abyss has indeed opened, but heaven has opened as well. It is when everything else hides itself that God appears; when all beside fails us, that God imparts himself.

Ah! if to escape such tortures I had to renounce such joys; if, in order not to be touched by blame or disquieted by anxiety, I must never have tasted the rapture of that humiliation which Jesus exalts, of that sadness which he consoles, of that gloom which truth suddenly irradiates,—I should turn away from such negative happiness, I should leave those regions where there is neither night nor day. I should go to seek and find my God where he is, in life, despite all the dangers and accidents with which that life is fraught.

But there is more still. In attaching myself to truth, I have bid farewell to success. I have submitted to the ridicule that attends unsuccessful causes; condemned myself to the regrets of causes lost ; that which possesses my whole heart meets with nothing but contempt; I spend my life in supporting interests about to perish. My future sinks with the frail skiff to which I have unwisely trusted it. Men will laugh at what extorts my tears, will scoff at the object of my reverence. Not that that would so much signify, but truth herself seems only to win mere skirmishes ; she loses pitched battles ; no flourishes of trumpets for her, still less fortune ; they who become her courtiers must be ready to live upon little. Ill clothed, ill fed themselves, they must make up their minds to see her beaten, wandering hither and thither, repulsive through her wounds, and yet they must love her. Slow are her advances ; true, what she once has conquered she retains ; century by century she takes an onward step, and never recedes. Yet is this so certain ? At all events, if she takes a hundred years for this step in advance, I, for my part, only take fifty or sixty to vanish from the scene. If **I assist** at the departure, I seldom can be **present** at the arrival. Each time that she falls, that I see her weak, that impious hands press forward to crush her ; each time that shouts of joy greet one of her defeats, that humanity scoffs at her, that those, even, who once recognised and for a season served, deny and curse her ; when it seems as though she were about to die,—then my soul too dies within me.

But, as I have told you, as soon as earth departs heaven draws near ; banished from time, eternity is left me. It is there I shall behold thee, Truth— thou, the despised one ! There thou wilt shine forth in thy perfect beauty. There no one will mistake thee more ! Thou wilt fill immensity ! No lie will dare to show its rags in thy presence. Sovereign, triumphant, oh how the contemplation of thee then will blot out all former misery !

Yes, I love you, beautiful, unsuccessful causes ; I love you, little, despised minorities. Where there are but few, they draw closer to each other. For-lorn hopes have their glad days. Have we not mutually pressed hands beneath the fire of the batteries ? In the bivouac, it is true, the peaceful images of a quiet life have passed before our eyes ; have they never appeared to us in the very thick of the battle ? The good soldier delights in war ; war gives him his brother-in-arms.

And besides, if the lovers of truth feel sadness,

the courtiers of error are not always joyous. After
all, it is cold in the fog. Argumentative intellects
are sometimes weary of neutral shades and half
convictions. Utilitarianism has its thorns; expe-
diency is not always so convenient as it seems.
Truth never bends, I allow; but doubt bends out of
season. A belief may be an obstacle; but a compromise is not always a facility. There are many
times in life when the wise would pay dear for a
little of that folly by means of which the enthu-
siastic soul overleaps at one bound the impossibilities that facts oppose to it.

He who takes a high flight is in danger of falling;
he who drags himself along the ground knocks
himself against every stone, and gets entangled
in every briar.

Do you know the ideal? Then you know
sorrow too.

Existence has an iron hand; she leads us
whither we would not; and when we are about to
mount some of those fairy cars whose habit it is
to travel in the clouds, she abruptly unharnesses,
puts our steed back in the stable, closes the door,
takes the key, and sends us about our business.
Then, while we labour at our vocation, and dark
hours succeed to colourless hours; then, while we
are seen trotting along the turnpike-road, each of

our steps raising the dust, our head low and our
eye extinct; then, all the while another self has
risen far away from earth, it has found the regions
where music echoes round, where thought is
queen, and to will is to create. Look closely and
you will see those lands all bathed in light which
float above the poorest lives. Legends tell us of
the hippogriff; it is the steed of paladins and
princes; we, who are neither princes nor paladins,
we have the ideal. We mount, and then, at once
we have got out of the frozen regions, have escaped
our prison gloom; we cleave the air, we reach
home, that wondrous home, where everything is
waiting for us and every one loves us. That is
indeed the true fatherland which our thoughts
inhabit. Oppressed down below, contradicted,
mortified, here the heart dilates. There we were
slaves, we were bored, we had no energy, and
scarcely any wishes. Here life is radiant, everything charms and inspirits; we are free, we take
possession of ourselves, ideas command, facts obey;
we become once more the head of creation.

And do not suppose that these vast flights weary
the soul; that, having felt so keenly, it returns exhausted; that, dazzled with the splendours of that
imaginary world, the poverty of a prosaic existence
re-seizing, paralyses it. So long as space remains
open; so long as it can plod on, and yet set out

toward those radiant spheres, leave them, return
to them, weave golden threads between one land
and the other, you have nothing to fear. Being a
planet, it is good to have a sun.

Go ask for harvests from those miserable worlds,
fixed on the extreme verge of a disproportioned
orbit, far from the star that gives light and heat,
and they will point you to the unmeasurable distance hardly traversed by a pale ray. They wander
on in their twilight; they accomplish their cycle.
Ask from them nothing more. But when the earth
is placed beneath the direct rays of the sun, then
concerts break out, flowers open, myriads of creatures are born and flutter with joy. It is the time
of harvest; the fair season when the reapers lay
the golden corn, and granaries overflow, and trees
bend beneath their fruit. All creatures rejoice in
their being, the poor are warm, the hungry eat
at will.

Believe me, the man who has never met with the
ideal, has a dull eye and a wrinkled brow. He
stoops over the narrow furrow, watered drop by
drop by his sweat and his tears; he grows old
before the time; his hands let fall, before the
evening comes, the implements that have become
too heavy. The families from which the ideal is
banished as a suspicious interloper, will be very
well organized, I allow; they will have a prudent

demeanour; you will not find any sudden sallies
or extravagances there; but they will produce
nothing remarkable; the children will never give
any of those shouts of delight which make the
house thrill; you will see none of that beauteous
fervour that gives colour to the cheek; nor that
fire that flashes lightning from the eye; there
will be no rush to storm an idea, none of those
bursts of energy, and those feats of prowess by
which the soul rules and bends the actual to
its will.

You are going to tell me that if one soars so high
one runs the risk of falling back broken to pieces;
I have experienced this. But what of that? voyages
are conquests. What I have seen belongs to me
henceforth, and, wounded though I be, I am ir-
rational enough to prefer my bruises, with my
memories, to the small health of a valetudinarian
walking safely round and round his own court-
yard.

When the ideal is torn away from us, it is indeed
a part of our own selves that we lose. When the
golden   roll upon their hinges; when a sword
flames on the threshold of Eden; when, instead
of all those singing voices, a silence prevails; when
we must return exiled to the earth, that has lost
those luminous reflections sent down from higher
spheres; when we meet with our impoverished

selves; when we wake dis-illusioned,—the heart contracts, a terror falls upon us; it is a reverse indeed; our royal robes are changed for tatters; we were walking as conquerors; we have to labour at the wheel.

But at least I have lived, I have reigned, for a season I have cast off the yoke. I have traversed the universe as a ruler. I have been poet, musician, philosopher. I have sown liberty broadcast in every latitude. Nations have been stirred by the tones of my voice; slaves have broken their chains; family life has been elevated; the gospel has regenerated the world. I have enjoyed the happiness of heaven. Would I consent to have possessed nothing, that I might have nothing to regret?

Besides, if I am on the ground I shall get up again. Covered with rags, I have but to stretch out my hands once more to grasp the purple. God be praised, it is with the ideal as with monarchs. The king is dead; long live the king!

But we have no longer to deal with dreams. It is a positive sadness that now awaits me.

Work is there before me. I have chosen it; I love it supremely; it is my dignity, my strength. As friend answers friend, even so it meets my aspirations; my existence derives its value from it. The hours were slow, now they fly. I felt a void that nothing filled; now everything within me is awake and stirs.

Oh, joy supreme of meeting with thought, of giving it a form, a voice; of sending it forth glowing with youth, thrilling with the impulse of flight through free space; there is in it something of the Creator!

One had felt the spirit of life gushing up within; it craved for air, and see, it lives indeed, it soars! Here, all alone, I have placed foot within the domains of eternal light. How beautiful, how divine the joy I feel! Drag on, monotonous days; pile up your difficulties, heavy claims of duty; blow, contrary winds; reality, rear thy mountains in my path; I will traverse you with flaming brow; I will lift you without my arm giving way; I defy, I laugh at you all.

For I must needs fight hard, and this is only an added pleasure. I would not accept an easy success. I disdain the prize that costs me little. Those tame, slow-winged thoughts, captured as soon as seen; those commonplace beauties within reach of the first comer, would ill satisfy the ardour of conquest which I feel.

Well spoken that! It proves a generous spirit and a manly vigour. Now is the time. Creative intellect, imagine and shape. Fight hard, thou

N

good soldier! Launch forth thy ship, bold navigator, and discover new worlds!

Woe is me! everything flies away and escapes me. I did see; now I can no longer clearly distinguish aught. There were vivid colours; they are all drowned in mist. I did know what I meant to say; it spoke itself within me; the tones vibrated, the exact words were there; now I neither know nor comprehend anything. Once, whatever it was I wanted to express, I felt it at least,—felt love, hatred, agitating emotions; now all are frozen up; my arteries seem scarcely to beat. I make one last attempt; I lose breath; I cannot succeed in warming myself.

My mind is void, my vein is exhausted, my faculties are dead. Mad I was; imbecile I am; unprofitable I shall be! If at least the folly of my desires had departed from me! If I had but the common sense of the ass! he never dreams of headlong speed; he is not indignant at not bleeding beneath the golden spur of the Arabian courser; no burst of martial music could ever make him rear under the switch of the boor who is dragging him along. But I,—I, who am incapable, am also ambitious; I have that absurd combination of great aspirations and small powers; a giant in desire, I am a pigmy in action; an absurd creature all compounded of inflation and impotence.

And yet this suffering of mine is a noble suffering after all. No; it is not celebrity, it is not applause, that I seek. Enamoured of the ideal, I only aspire to its possession. Let that shine forth, and I am content to get out of sight. Obscurity pleases me. I find it fraught with ineffable graces.

My desire was a very simple one. To find my vocation ; to send forth my conviction ready armed to take its chance at the tournament ; mysterious messages to souls that weep and love as I do ; to interchange with those unknown friends words of sympathy ; mutually to point to the sky ; to press hands. That was all I desired. God, who had given me the hope, takes it away ; the azure he had unfolded above me is clouded over ; he had rapt me from earth, he lets me fall down there again. My God, I submit.

The moment that word has left my lips, I feel myself relieved. So soon as my heart is humbled, it recovers its peace. True power, divine creativeness, lies after all in making one's own soul obedient.

My grief becomes dear to me. If I had not caught a glance of celestial splendour, would my soul retain these reflections of them ? There are sadnesses more precious than certain joys.

And then I belong to the God of compassions. Seeing me cast down, he comes and abides with me. God resists the proud; the broken spirit attracts him. Now that I begin to know and to hope nothing more from self, God lifts me up, he tears away the cerements ; my eyes open once more ; I hear the harmonies of old ; my wings are restored ; God has given me back the ideal.

But this is not all.

You want to do good : one is less than a man without this. I promise you sadness. Each effort of yours will bruise itself against the inertia of general indifference. Contrary views will run full tilt against your good intentions. Be useless, nay, be wicked if you will, you have the world and the devil on your side. Be a Christian, act like a believer ; hell, earth, and I was almost about to say heaven, will array themselves against you.

For God requires men of war; he delights in souls of proof,—strong, enduring, and it is by hard blows he forges these. You think, perhaps, that because you have taken up God's cause, everything is to grow easy before you ! But when have great captains spared battles to their soldiers ? Obstacles, oppositions, resistance of inert matter, passions of prejudiced minds, nay, even the consciences of the best souls will range themselves against you.

The privilege of serving God has to be bought,

to be paid for. Once enrolled in that ever-advancing army, one must bid adieu to self-indulgence. No elegant idleness, no good-society indifference, no heart-selfishness will do for the soldier. He must relinquish all the pleasant careless ease of a life without toil and without purpose. Interests of the first order take possession of the mind, and put a bridle in the mouth. We become the bondmen of an idea. It has rights over us; God, who has intrusted it to our care, will inquire of us what we have done with it.

Nothing so easy as to let souls lose themselves; people go to ruin; orphans wander at random; the poor get hopelessly embarrassed; the vicious sink down into debauchery; every one goes to destruction in his own way,—this is done of itself. The moment you rise in rebellion against this law of gravitation, in virtue of which whatever inclines to the abyss falls into the abyss,—you have the whole weight of the avalanche on your arms.

The man that you have recovered from a course of depravity, loves it, and plunges back. That family whom you are seeking to raise by occupation, persists in crouching in idleness. The child whom you have snatched from the pestilential atmosphere, carries its fatal germs within; as he grows older, the disease develops.

And if it is not a human creature, if it is some

cause you are full of, why, every one else has one of his own, with its difficulties and cares. Do not expect another to give his heart to your undertaking.

You sacrifice your time to it, good; you devote your money to it, it is your duty so to do. Now then, it will surely advance in conformity with the gospel, and beneath the protection of God? Yes, God protects, but God also tries. You thought you had nothing more to do but to fold your arms; self-seeking, even in your devotedness, you were to be interested up to this point, and no further; something of pride had stepped into your zeal; it seemed to you, that when once the work was set agoing, the task of consolidating it belonged to God; that God ought to be honoured by your offerings; that he ought to take care of his own cause; that henceforth you had nothing to do but to inhale the perfume of its good report. Oh, how mistaken you were! At its first setting out, your bark has run upon the breakers. All the difficulties of this world are on its lee! Sometimes your undertaking lacks proper direction; sometimes the very object for which it was intended seems to escape from view.

Working on without purpose or result, it reminds one of machinery which (the mills having ceased work) has to be kept going at great expense for fear rust should spoil it; or else, ill managed, not managed at all, your enterprise comes to a stand-still for want of a proper head.

Then it is that you will know what care and dis-couragement really are. Then, too, you will know what prayer is, and humiliation on our bended knees, and the cry that brings God out from his sanctuary.

Without dejection, you would not know deliver-ance. Without this sadness, would you have ex-perienced this joy?

But if the originating an enterprise fatigues, much more does the anxiety for a soul's salvation torture us.

The age may deny it if it will; but it is a materialist age. Only listen to the laughter pro-voked by that one little word—conversion. Look at the ridicule that is poured on any young girl who pretends to love for eternity, the one she loves in time.

What! earth does not suffice you, then! You have got ten, twenty years of enjoyment before you, and that is not enough! You are so utterly absurd and visionary, that the affection of a worthy sceptic cannot satisfy you! Your heart, withered by the fire of a narrow-minded pros-elytism, prefers to languish, solitary, broken, obedient to the tyranny of I know not what sort of principle, to beating freely against the heart that had given itself to you. It is insanity, it is almost wickedness.

Well then, thank God, there are some of these insane souls, these wicked beings. There are women who cherish the immortal in the man they love; they are so frenzied and so cruel that they would give all their blood, give the happiness of ten lives, in order that he might be eternally happy! In vain would you hold out to them a prosperous existence; they know that death would cut it all short. There, where they go, their beloved must go with them. The thought of a love severed on the threshold of paradise makes them shudder with horror. They cannot understand a happiness compatible with an irrevocable separation. They have the selfishness to desire passionately, exclusively, that their loved one should not be lost. They have the paltry ambition of inquiring whether he possesses God! Aided by prayer, sustained by faith, illuminated by the splendour of truth, they would—haunted by that desire of dominion common to feeble creatures,—they would that the power of prayer, the security of faith, should fortify his soul; that a royalty should be given to it; that the one they love, assuming his proper place, should be everywhere in advance of themselves,—their guide, their support, their master everywhere.

Nor are women alone in this their delirium.

What is that young rich man doing, he upon whom all earth smiles? He is praying. For what? For a companion with whom he may pray.

That father, that mother, wherefore is it that they have fallen on their knees? Oh, do you not already know? Their child has a soul; that soul may suffer much, but it can never die. Their child may become a Christian, but he may also be a castaway. He may, perhaps, be a loyal, generous man; a champion of liberty, an originator of ideas, a performer of great and noble actions; perhaps a mere sybarite, an idler, an egotist, a debauchee —one of the lost !

Believe me, if the supplications that rise from earth to heaven could become suddenly visible, you would count by myriads those prayers that wrestle for the salvation of souls.

We have known them; they have stirred within us, they have consumed us. My child ! sometimes that is all we can say, but Jesus understands us. Oh, let me die, so only he be saved. He will not listen to me. My God, he will listen to thee. He distrusts me; send him thy Spirit of love, thy prevailing Spirit, that Spirit that may not be resisted. If thou wilt, I will never see him more ;

but let me have him in heaven ! My God ! What ! again a fall ! Hast thou indeed permitted it ? Seest thou not that he is about to escape from thee ?

And night and day these hands are uplifted, these eyes drowned in tears look up without cessation. These are inexpressible anguishes, but who among us would consent to miss them ? When you lay her new-born babe in her arms, does the mother regret having suffered ? Or even if she must die, may one not say to her, as to Rachel : Fear not, thou hast a son ?

But now I come upon a strange form of sorrow. My expanded soul takes cognisance of the woes of the whole world ; a terror of them seizes upon me, and, as it were, a shame of living in such an accursed place.

There are hours when time and distance are done away with. Past centuries come, and bring me wave on wave the fragments of all their shipwrecks. The long perspective does not hide from me a single agony. Those wrecks, those corpses, those poor mutilated forms, witnesses to human atrocity, bleed as they did on that distant day ; those discoloured lips murmur words of indignation and of vain imploring.

You exclaim that all these people, one way or other, are dead and gone ! You have no tears to spend upon mummies, forsooth ! You have no notion of weeping for the death of a Chinaman! What though some have been quartered, sawn in twain, built up alive ; though humanity should have been in all ages intoxicated with cruelty, should have sought its supreme excitements in supreme tortures ; that is nothing to you ; let every one bear his own burden,—this is none of yours. And calmly, sometimes with a smile upon your lips, you can reflect upon these infamous scenes.

We may have absurd refinements perhaps, the sensitiveness of a poor weak woman ; but when history opens before us her polluted book ; when the cries of the butchered, the howls of the broken on the wheel rise from those pages, you negligently turn over ; when we see the polite and reputable society of great epochs enjoying the death-rattle of a Damiens, torn by red-hot pincers, torn limb from limb, slowly, deliberately, that the pleasure may not come too soon to an end, a horror comes over me, a horror of our human nature.

You may say what you like ; this does concern us.

That a King of Dahomey should have baths of blood prepared, that he should send his hideous hordes to massacre whole villages, to bring him thousands of victims; that these diabolical customs should be celebrated every year! Pooh! those heads are woolly, black, all that goes on in Africa! If we were to fret over every choice supper cannibals may make, or over the summary justice of Zulus and Persians, or negroes sold wholesale, or missionaries strangled in Japan, or even over murders committed in Europe, why, our lives would not be worth holding.

Our lives are rendered less agreeable, I allow, but nevertheless it is not a matter of choice, and everybody cannot be deaf at will. I, for my part, both hear and see; I breathe in that jail with those that kill and are killed, and I feel myself stifling there.

It is all the same to you perhaps, that, under the pretext of surprising the secrets of pain, science should dissect living, panting, creatures. God has made them, you hold, for the scalpel, for ill usage, made them to amuse men by the spectacle of their agonies. We believe the very reverse: we are lacerated, we are revolted.

Corruption too afflicts us as much as cruelty disgusts. We cannot look on without tears at the pitiable pleasures of those poor creatures who drag their weariness from one debauch to another; who think they enjoy life because they pollute it; who parade their sadness beneath carnival tinsel,— tired, disgusted, satiated with vice, their heart dead, their soul sinking beneath the contempt it feels, and the repulsion it inspires.

However closely we may wall ourselves round by our selfishness, there is always some chink which admits the smell of blood. A cry of despair may sound through it too. We are not master of our own sight ; a random glance may meet very disagreeable spectacles.

Well, but what does all this lead to?

To very little ;-merely to praying and working. A heart is but a small thing. Take care : a heart-beat shall revolutionize the world ! These little ones who kneel are they to whom God says, Forward ! and barbarous laws crumble away ; religious liberty by a touch breaks prison-doors and galley-slaves' chains ; whole nations rise kindled by a common compassion ; men give their lives to destroy slavery, their money to feed the hungry, their time to instruct the masses.

The powerful once employed his strength in torturing the weak ; now he puts out all his energy to defend him. Animals are protected ; society is revolted at massacres, their geographical position makes no difference. No soul can fall without other souls suffering. When the poor are cold, the rich shiver. A breath of charity has passed over the earth. The blood of a common Father begins once more to circulate in our veins.

These men of tears are found the men of action ;
if they did not weep, nothing would be done.

Often, it is true, when the pestilent miasmas of
vice rise and surround us, we feel a desire to
depart. Just as the swallows at the first cold of
autumn begin to try their wings, assemble, and
then take flight to serener shores, so we too would
fain set out on our journey heavenwards.

There is in this sense of disquietude and agitation, as it were, a giant's effort to free himself
from his bonds. The sum of human woe, the
aggregate of crime, weighs upon the soul ; it bears
a world, a burden which we must cast down before
God, under pain of being crushed beneath it.

When one cannot banish from one's mind the
crimes and the griefs of men ; when one refuses to
be consoled about them ; when that heavenly
home-sickness seizes the heart, yes, it is very true,
one would willingly give way to indolent languor.
The mind might easily lose itself in a morbid contemplation of evil. The soul might yield to the
inertia of passive regrets. Aspiration, that force ·
of all elect natures, may become their weakness as
well. It is a dazzling void in which vigour may
be submerged. The moment we are contented
with such a mood, it becomes fatal. They who
allow assassinations have blood on their own

hands ; our effeminacies, however lachrymose they may be, will never prevent one crime ; Satan encourages them, they intoxicate conscience.

But I assure you that, because the eyes are dry, it does not follow that the heart is valiant. To remain cold is a very different thing from becoming energetic. To feel nothing is not the best condition for action. No one will go and seek the diamond in the dark of the mine, you will not brave the underground depths, will not snatch the stone from its matrix, unless you are haunted by the passion for diamonds.

Morbid sadness, you exclaim, morbid and useless ! Nay, beautiful sadness ! It is through this alone that man attains to progress.

But I will show you another which will seem to you even more chimerical,—sadness because of my sins.

I have received the gospel, and my conduct contradicts the gospel. I love God, and yet I disobey God. I desire eternal life, and I am unworthy of eternal life. I know God, and I remain far from him. I would glorify my king ; I dishonour him. My faith, my piety, my happiness, should attract loyal souls to the truth ; my doubts, my faults, down to the very sufferings of my divided heart, repel them, and restore them to the

world.   If, walking at Christ's side, I could but
enjoy the restoring rapture of full communion with
him !   O Holy Spirit, I sigh after thee ! I want
thy help, and I know not how to ask for it.   I call
thee, and see, I am afraid of thy answering me ! I
desire thee, and when thou comest, I grieve thee.
How long shall I languish, half conqueror, half
conquered ; my heart now full of thee, now full of
the world ?

O my sadness, I bless thee ! Thou savest me
from myself ! Thanks to thee, I cannot succeed
in taking the shadow for the substance. Whatever
else he gives to me, if Jesus gives himself not, I
count mere dross.   Thou allowest me neither
compromise nor cowardice.   Thou hast aroused
in me the desire of perfection, it torments me to
my salvation.   .

This may appear to you a mania—almost an
insanity ! The wisdom which enjoins us to proportion our ambition to our power condemns such
audacity ; it is only ill-balanced minds that permit
themselves such dreams ; this mirage both results
from their ignorance, and causes their torment :
men of sense limit their desires ; they only covet
on the condition of possessing. Perhaps, however,
we too we shall possess.

Our sadness is the earnest of an inheritance.
In this we are wise ; in this we judge well, that

what we want we shall assuredly have. Where we purpose to go, most surely we shall go one day. Desires are the aërial road that lead to the skies. Desires once dead, the soul is dead too. The impetuosity of desire takes heaven by force. Desire that renders prayers fervent and indefatigable will hasten—it is God that tells us so—the triumphant return of Jesus. Desire has dominion over souls; it reigns on high. My desire makes me suffer; my desire makes me a king. I will keep suffering, and will keep desire.

Have you ever heard Mendelsohn's Lobgesang? If so, you remember that gloom brooding over the world, and that voice rising through the silence with accents of despairing energy. You hear those groans that wander through the solitudes, and that cry of the earth in distress, which pierces the air, traverses space, and shakes the skies: 'When will the night be past?'

Above the tumult of nature, above the clash of weapons, in tears, as beneath laughter, we hear it still. This is the cry of all tender, all broken hearts; of all who are unhappy, all who believe themselves happy. This is what the insane keep calling aloud, what the wise murmur, what perhaps even the fallen, the lost soul repeats unconsciously; this is the language of the seekers after truth, the lovers of the ideal ; the shuddering question of lamentable sadness, the hope-thrilled sigh of sadness which is beautiful.

It is only the sad who have these vehemencies of aspiration.

Then after an interval which makes our pulse stand still, as though emptiness prevailed, — as though in all the ruined universe there was nothing that could reply to that supreme invocation, —a transport of victory bursts forth ; the choir of angels fills the air ; words, light, all ray out at once.

The night is past ! this is what they proclaim. The night is past, the day is here !

VII

DEATH.

A S I sit writing, the lake stretches out before my eyes, calm, slate-coloured, in that pristine morning peace and freshness that no other hour of the day will restore to it.　There is hardly a wrinkle to disturb the transparency of the surface ; hardly one of those long, slow undulations—caused, one would say, by some sigh from the deep heart of the waters—to rise gently, and, swelling on from distance to distance, come at last to wet the little pebbles on the shore.　The snowy mountains, half folded in mist, rather allow their pyramids to be guessed than seen ; the opposite side still sleeps beneath the vapours that muffle every sound. A boat approaches languidly and leisurely; its two large sails have met some wandering breath, they are slightly swelled ; their exact triangle stands

out against the soft background ; the one catching
the light is white and dazzling as an angel's wing ;
the other, entirely in shade, is grey and dull, and
the limpidity of the water reflects alike—just dis-
turbing them with a slight shiver—both the bright
and the sombre outline.

It seems to me as though that boat were bearing
my life away.

Thus it is that we too glide on, one wing in the
light, another in the shade. When night comes—
before then, perhaps—those folded sails will no
longer go in quest of the breeze ; the bright sun
will no longer shine on them ; the passing cloud,
the gloom of the dull day will touch them no more ;
they will not have left the faintest image on the
depths that once reflected them ; not a ripple of
the water will tell of their passage ; other boats
will come, then others ; they too will disappear ;
while the lake will keep its eternal beauty.

At the age of twenty, death does not alarm ; we
have never seen a person die. Besides, the unknown reigns here as well as there ; to advance in
life, to recede towards death, both are alike to
journey to new and undiscovered lands. The caravan sets out, the travellers beckon : Power is with
us, they cry ; with us the varied chances of adven-
ture ; hasten, take part with us in festivals, in vic-

tories; we are strong, we are joyous! But see, their
eyes have wept, their face is sad; wrinkles furrow
the brow of those victors; that laugh of theirs
has a false ring; and while they press on, and fill
the air with clamour, other voices suddenly begin to
sound. Divinely pure in tone, they tell the sweet
deaths of those whom Jesus has early called home.
These went in the serenity of their morning; they
had seen the flowers open, they had not seen them
wither; they had inhaled the fresh air of the dawn,
the heat of the noon-day sun did not beat on their
heads; their love for God had known no treachery;
Jesus, whom they soon met with, took them by the
hand; they followed him with all their heart, which
they had entirely given. They dwell in radiant
habitations; theirs is the burning fervour, the swift
obedience of the seraphim; they know, they love,
they work, as do the angels. In the plenitude of
liberty, in the possession of all their energies, they
glorify God. These too say, Come!

The young man listens. Such voices have a
charm that the others lacked; we feel that truth
vibrates therein; they bring light with them. If
God willed, how readily should we go where they
call!

Nevertheless life continues, years pass, the caravan pursues its way; one has taken rank, one
marches in the midst of the cohort, of the uproar,

in the very thick of the encounter. To get on, to fight at need, to divide the spoil, this gives one abundance to do. There is little beside the tumult of the camp to be heard. One works hard and suffers; the place one occupies has not been gained without trouble; the question is, how to keep it. These very efforts and sufferings have their charm. We feel that we live; we acquire— know what we have—lay stress upon it; greatly, indeed, because of what it has cost us, more even, perhaps, than because of what it gives. Never mind. Go, tell the soldier engaged in a victorious onslaught to leave his regiment, to retrace his steps, to take his way down there towards those uncertain horizons.

In middle life, very frequently heaven veils itself from us. It had opened out, it closes again; it had seemed to us familiar, it grows strange now; it had been our country far more than the earth, now it recedes in unfathomable perspective. Our thought, which used to dwell there for a while, keeps coming and going; then it grows used to remain here below, soon it requires an effort to rise; such flights exhaust it; they grow rarer, shorter, happy if indeed they are still attempted. I do not mean by this that the Christian in the plenitude of his faculties forgets God; no, it is to God that he consecrates his vigour, he serves in

the army of the great Captain; but if he walks
with God, still it is upon this earth that he walks.
The labourer may sometimes, indeed, think of the
evening; but it is his work that above all engrosses
him; he delights in action; the day is fair, let us
make the most of the day; when the shades of
twilight gather, why then we will look upon the
side of night.

When we are young, death does not surprise us;
in middle life, at that season of energy which is,
as it were, a protest against immobility, it amazes;
we can no longer comprehend it. Shall we grow
more familiar with it later, when the rapid current
will have left us to drift on shore; when successes
will be achieved without us; when the travelled
road will lie far beyond us; when all movement
will desert us; when, in that great journey towards
the future, we shall only be able to keep up with
such as are wounded; to sympathize with the
broken in heart? I do not know. It may be so.
If habit has but more firmly riveted the chains that
bind us to this world, on the other hand, sorrows
have strained them. In our Father's house are
many loved ones, who wait for us. We have recovered the rising road; our affections lead us
back to it, our memories make it dear to us. And
then Jesus may with one stroke dispel the clouds,
and as soon as heaven is seen, we tend towards it.

Nevertheless, here we are now, living, vigorous, active. Affections beam round us; our soul possesses all its faculties, and all are in full exercise; each morning finds us well and strong; each brings us some pleasant occupation; there is delight in existence. Useful and earnest, fraught with poetry as well, life has its frank gaiety; it has its emotions of sad and tender sort. The heart beats high; good gets done; one is reminded of that exuberance of a summer day, when from dawn to evening, and even on into the early watches of the night, the busy reapers bind the sheaves; when the fields shout aloud by the voice of their myriads of happy creatures; when the birds sing with all their little might beneath every tree; when the sun flames, and after he has sunk below the mountain the vault of heaven still glows, and the starry depths vibrate, sparkle, and shoot their fire-arrows without a pause.

At such a moment of our life; after one of these energetic days, in that first deep and complete sleep which comes to those who have worked hard, has it ever happened to you to be abruptly wakened up by a thought? An unusual thought which has seized hold of you, as a rough hand might do suddenly laid upon your shoulder. Death! that was what you thought; you were sleeping, you were full of trust, you had prayed to God; nay, you had

even committed your soul to him; he might retake
it if he willed, you had said this in all sincerity.
Death! nothing but that word; you grow cold.
God has disappeared, faith has disappeared, death
stands before you alone, hideous.

My heart will cease to beat! I feel it there
under my hand; it will. be felt no longer. My
breath, the fresh air that brings me life, it will have
been exhaled for ever. My eyes will grow dim;
this hand will be cold as ice, they will shut me up
in a coffin, they will nail me down; and there
within it, under the earth,—far from all my own
people, from those who love me, whom I love,—
terrible changes will go on which will make me an
object of horror. How will this happen to me,
when, where? What agony shall I have to go
through? What shall I feel at that supreme moment when respiration ceases? Will life hover in
me vaguely still? Shall I see the tears shed
around me, shall I hear sobs, will my paralysed
mouth receive kisses without any power to testify
that I am still there?

All this that is fraught with darkness comes over
me. A fear paralyses me; so much the more
oppressive that I am without defence. My convictions, my hope, my will, remain in a state of
torpor. I undergo the pressure of a force against
which my benumbed faculties cannot re-act.

I receive images. I am passive because disarmed.

Yes, but wait awhile ; I am going to tear the veil, to break the chain, to find myself again, my whole unbroken self! Death, I fear thee no more. I am a believer! My Master has bruised thy head! Thou mayest swallow me up, I live in thy despite. Eternity belongs to me. Thou shalt not even retain a particle of that dust into which thou hast reduced my body. And now, waking or asleep, do what thou wilt, thou canst do only what my God shall will.

There are certain poor souls who all their life long linger in these shadows of sleep. Without hope, as without defence, they go to meet death burdened with the fear of it.

But has this world then, indeed, so much to hold us back? What spell, what enchantment does it cast over us, that old, sad, dis-illusionized, we should be in love with it still? Have we not wept enough, even in the fairest life ; have not our sins wearied us enough ; our hearts deceived us ; have we not sufficiently touched the bottom of what once seemed unfathomable ; have not the iron bars, that cross each other in the embrasure of every loop-hole—realities antagonistic yet irremovable,—have not these crushed us back often

enough when we would fain have taken our flight
toward the pure azure that fills the sky! Alas!
we have bestowed little happiness, we have disappointed many hopes, have accomplished scarcely
any good, have rarely prevented evil! Look
where I will, I see sadness. Remorse rises with
the sorrows of the past; the present wearies
me. And shall I fear the future which shows
me the goal?

I fear it because it does not show me the goal!
I fear it because I have perhaps no Saviour, and
then I have no place on high. Perhaps there is
no eternal life. Perhaps I go into the undefined,
the vague, into those gloomy regions where life
may not enter. Shadows wander there, they are
gloomy, and keep their faces turned towards the
dear familiar earth; you hear the sound of sobs.
Is there a heaven down there, is there a God, is
there activity? Shall I find anything better than
what I must leave behind me? Will those who
remain after me rejoin me where I go? And I
myself, what shall I be; must I wander a phantom
amidst phantoms? If so, my misery is unspeak-
able, and I do well to be afraid.

Little pleased to live, trembling to die, bruised,
ever dreading fresh wounds, I bring myself down
to mere existence. I avoid all that warms; for it
might burn me; I forbid myself every impulse;

pro: who stirs runs a chance of accidents; I con-
thcentrate myself in self; I take care of myself;
not so much because I am anxious to last, as
reluctant to come to an end.

One soon finds them out these poor creatures
devoted to their own conservation. They watch
themselves, spy themselves; they will not allow
themselves this nor that, for death is here, it lurks
there, it has an eye upon them, and the great point,
the only point in short, is not to die.

Wrapped up in themselves, dragging on one
day after the other; let their wan face have one
wrinkle more this morning than it had yesterday;
let one pulsation more strike upon the finger that
questions the wrist; let an occurrence of any
kind shake that wadded abode where they keep
crouched, sheltered from life in order to live a
little longer, and there they are in consternation.
A terror comes over them, an irritation. People
want to kill them, they shall certainly die. Look
at their anxious eyes, their agitated features; the
poor soul condemned to the torture of a fixed
idea,—To live; and its life one that necessarily
dwindles, that oozes out from every crack, that is
on the point of extinction, and then tell me whether
there be a more miserable sadness than this.

The recklessness of the sceptic terrifies me, but
it does not occasion me the same repulsion. It is

indeed madness, but in that very disdain of
that it inspires, there is a certain semblance of
generosity; even in the very contempt of death
that it imparts, one discovers, I know not what of
audacity, that better becomes the human soul than
the debility of terror.

He who is indifferent is not far from being
courageous. The excess of daring is almost an
excess of virility. One may hope everything from
him who remains a man. But fear and trembling
leave nothing behind them, the very individuality
melts away. What can be expected from a soul
when it has ceased to be?

Wonderful though it be, while death itself frightens
many, what follows death disturbs very few minds.

The condemned criminal shudders at the edge
of the axe. After that, do not require his thoughts
to reach any further!

One quails at the approaches of disease; the
anguish of the transition terrifies. How will death
strike; shall I have long to languish; or will an
unexpected blow cut short my life; will it fall
during sleep, or when I am awake? What shall I
feel? These thoughts come and go; they enter
in at every hour, they force themselves into all
places, there is no shaking them off. But the
holiness of God, the claims of God, his threats, his

promises—not those we have attributed to him, those he himself has made ;—our sins, our salvation,—who in that great day of accusation will be on our side, who will be against us ; if hell await us, if we are certain of pardon, these facts, the only ones of importance, are cared for by a very small number. And yet, when life shall crumble away, these will remain, and we shall no longer see anything beside them.

Ah ! the dread of dying before one has found Jesus, is a reasonable dread indeed, and I should shudder not to find it in a soul. The misery of living without God admits of no consolation ; the horror of dying without a Redeemer allows neither deceitful illusions nor forgetfulness, nor anything whatever to divert the heart from it. This sadness must absolutely be laid before God ; absolutely it must be removed by him, by him and not another. Woe to us if we have never felt anything of the kind ! Let us petition for this incomparable suffering ; let the love of Jesus cast these terrors across our path ; let these furies pursue us, tear us, urge us on, on to the feet of Christ, on till in our desolation the cry escape from our breasts : I am lost ! Come thou to my aid ?

Would it indeed be possible to despair of a despairing soul ? The souls that appal us are the souls at ease. Those who doubt of their salvation

because they detest their own ways, these are
seeking God. Nothing diverts them from this
search. They cannot be long deceived. They
imperatively need truth; even at their last hour
they will find it. But minds disturbed by no
doubts; grieved by no remorse; tormented by no
questions; souls that allow themselves to be borne
onwards by pleasant dreams towards a comfortable
future,—the peace of these souls indeed makes
me tremble.

Be that as it may, death takes us.

Some die all at once; the sacrifice is wholesale.
Others die by degrees. Disease appears, invades
the frame like a calm tide which rises slowly, but
for all that keeps rising. Our active faculties grow
paralysed. Existence shrinks; our circle is nar-
rowed; we can no longer do anything for others;
soon we can no longer do anything for ourselves.
The pain that we have long borne wearies our
courage, wears out that stock of energy and that
good moral health upon which invalids live for a
season. It wears out other things as well; perhaps the freshness of sympathy; perhaps the affections of those who love us. They pity us; oh, yes,
most certainly, and with all their heart; but here
are six months that they have been pitying us in
the same sort. Human springs give way when

the weight rests ever on the same place. One must not over-fatigue others; the best affection has its seasons of weariness. If we were to tell all our agonies, the burden that we impose upon our loved ones would grow heavier still. When a sigh escapes us, we see plainly that it gives pain, and we learn to be silent.

Concentrated sorrow soon turns to bitterness; our own excited sensibility affects our temper; the least thing hurts us; this is not attractive. A kind of constraint hampers our nearest, closest relations; on both sides the proper thing is said, but there is no more speaking as the heart prompts. The one studies hard to ask nothing, the other to give all; but there, where love once moved by uncalculating impulse, one feels the exercise of a self-possessed will. There was spontaneity, there is reflection.

And thus a separation takes place. Love had not permitted it; lassitude tolerates it. Dying day by day, one had kept one's-self hitherto alive by affection, present by thought; now we relinquish what escapes; we shun what is drawing away. Soon the hour comes when we think we see that even this little that we still are, is too much; that if one were to disappear for good and all, the first emotion over, there would be a certain sense of relief; that these other lives bent now over the sick-bed would regain their elasticity; that they would look more freely on the bright side of things; that one would be wept indeed, but little regretted. An infinite wretchedness takes possession of the soul, one of those torments that consume it. Incapable of living; little prepared to die; we remain a stranger in our own home, solitary amongst our family. It is an extreme case, and a rare torture perhaps; but, believe me, there are these sufferings in the poor heart which has long lived upon pity.

But a sudden illness swoops down upon us. No one guessed its extent. Our friends are calm about it; we are not so. We have felt the chill of death. It advances; others begin to stir around us. It advances still; they grow alarmed. And while it is gaining on us rapidly, surely, one distracted soul is looking out for its way.

Unless Jesus be standing by, it is horrible. For agony has seized upon us, and hardly leaves us power to think. Drowning men must experience something of the kind. The abyss summons us, our being escapes from itself, and the mind looks on, contemplates this inevitable, this near dissolution, that it has no power to prevent. The process is a rapid one. All that had charmed us recedes into faint distance; all that we thought we possessed crumbles away. Earth, life, are already so far from us that we can hardly discern a few of their flitting shadows.

How cold it is where we are going, how bare, how sad! It seems as though a mere void were opening out; nothing more that is familiar; nay, nothing whatever. Those we love are standing by, mute, alarmed,—they weep; but those tears seem to us already far off; the hour that takes us away puts between us and them an ever-increasing distance; it is but a faint accent that the last breezes of earth bear in upon our ear. We walk alone, ay, quite alone; most completely denuded of all, along that road whose end none can discern. No one,—not even thou whose pale face is more altered than my own,—no one comes with me. I hear them, they remain in the place inhabited by men; I,—I am swept away; I must go; darkness surrounds me.

All is over, life has passed; all that it showed were then only shadows. Where shall I grasp a reality? Give me something solid, something that lasts, something to hold by! Everything reels and flies away; I,—I am going; I sink; my flesh shudders, my soul refuses; some force sweeps me along; I can do nothing against it, how swift it is!

And then, like that sudden after-glow that re-kindles the flames on the snowy peaks, and gives

light to the mountain-sides that day has forsaken,—
in one instant, life, what I possessed, what I loved,
all comes back upon me with its first freshness. I
see you again, woods that I have so dearly loved ;
I feel your shade, a fragrance of wild flowers passes
over me ; I see you, garden walks I have so often
trodden, and that apple-tree that flowered in May.
All at once I hear the thousand sounds of the
country ; the glory of fine mornings beams round,
little children jumping with joy, old people—this
and the other—nod to me. Is there a sun there
where I go, and will my eyes see again what they
have just contemplated ?

But what am I doing, thus wasting my regrets ?
My husband, my children ! Nothing now but
that one cry ! They in despair without me, and
shall not I console them ? The soul about to
depart returns, wraps its loved ones round, ex-
hausts itself in a last effort. Accustomed to fore-
cast, it is still anxious ; it seeks to traverse that
sad road that its forsaken ones must henceforth
walk along alone ; it, sounds it,—oh how fain would
it ward away all its perils ! There is a snare here !
There a casualty ! The failing hand is raised to
warn. Alas ! the hour is come, and death will
not wait.

All at once our conscience, wakening with a
start, looks within. The past that had sent us

images now restores us facts. Words, actions, feelings, things acknowledged, things ignored, all live again. Oblivion has swallowed up nothing, time has weakened nothing. Evil is evil, sin is horrible, excuses fail, the holiness of God shines resplendent. We may once have doubted of God ; we are certain of God's holiness now ; nay, we even see it with superhuman clearness ; we comprehend it in its absolute character. It cannot be otherwise ; no virtue can stand in its sight, our iniquities are blasted, our righteousness effaced by its brightness, our mouths are closed by it. The whole world might cry in vain to us : Thou art mistaken ; we know now ; we have seen. Our soul possessed hitherto by so many passions, wearied with so many sadnesses, troubled with so many fears, feels only one thing now, that God is holy. Our heart finds in itself only terror—finds no love. To tremble is not to have faith. If paradise were to open out, should we indeed dare to cross its threshold ? Is our soul a fitting guest for paradise ? Has it met with Jesus when he walked on earth, despised of men ? Has it gone out towards him, given itself to him ; nay, did it even know him ?

For if it had known him, he would surely be there now ; Jesus never forsakes his own. To call him at this last hour ! the soul vaguely tries this,

he does not answer; he is only to be found by his
ransomed ones; that is very natural.

There is a Holy Spirit, an advocate of souls; he
may convert me. I ought not to have grieved him.
Besides, there is too little time now.

On the cross, it is true, there was little time
either, and yet the thief was saved. He was only
a thief. But I! I have resisted God, angered
him; I have hardened my heart; I willed it, I
chose it; I go where I ought to go. God himself
can do nothing for me.

Let us come out of the furnace.

I myself am but a poor creature; I have
offended my God far more than you; my conscience condemns me without mercy, and I have
nothing to say. If I went—I too—there where I
deserve to go, my portion would be darkness.
When I look in the direction of death, and consider what I am, I feel that I am afraid. When
my eyes wander over this beautiful earth, and fix
on the spot where graves are dug, I feel that I
grow sad. If I look on these loved faces; if my
hand meets that other hand which is mine, which
clasps me, which protects me, which has dried my
tears, my heart is ready to break. But I have my
stronghold where I take shelter, I have my rock
that I cling to; God is not far off, believe it on the

word of a poor feeble creature, and Jesus lets himself be found. I fall upon my knees; nay, there is not even any need for that; I speak to my God, I speak to my Saviour, I go just as my thoughts go. I tell him all my terror, and I reveal my wretchedness. A sin that I had not confessed would corrode my soul; a wicked state of mind that I had not laid just as it was before God, would oppress me with an insupportable burden. I ask for faith with all the forces of my being. I ask for pardon. I ask for a good life; I ask for a blessed death. I will not, O my God, go away in sadness; I will depart in the joy of thy salvation; I will press thy promises against my heart; I will leave behind m⬛brows all radiant with hope; I will not say Farewell; I will speak of our meeting again; I will feel the Holy Spirit, the Comforter, will have him to sustain me, him to quicken me. In proportion that she disengages herself, and that her earthly garments fall away, I will that wings should be given to my soul; I will to see the light beyond the dark and narrow valley; I will, O Jesus, that thou shouldest walk by my side. My loved ones cannot do this; they must remain behind; but as for thee, thou wilt surely be there; thou hast said it; thy staff supports, thy arm comforts me. I will that thou shouldest overthrow the enemy; thou wilt not let him approach me. I am weak ; thou knowest it well ; thou wilt never permit him those last, those horrible assaults. I will . . .

My God, have I indeed dared thus to speak. My God, I will what thou wilt.

All day long, my God is moved with compassion. Since the beginning of the world, not one sigh has ever lost its way between heaven and earth. If once I belong to God, he will prepare for me whatever is best.

I may ask everything. God has told me so. I have the liberty to desire. I have equal confidence in trusting my death to God as in submitting my life to him. From that moment I have peace, God knows what I wish ; if it is good for me, he will give it me.

Sudden or slow, easy or hard, death advances as God sends it ; nay, it is no longer death ; it is Jesus who comes to fetch me.

Provided that it be indeed He, and that I feel His presence, and confide my loved ones to His care ; the rest matters little.

Certainly it will be **He.**

VIII.

THE REASON WHY.

E are not destined to languish in unhappiness; it is not for this that God has created us. It is not followed by valetudinarian troops that Jesus the conqueror is to enter the skies, but at the head of valiant armies. His soldiers bear scars, it is true; but they have gained the battle; they are full of life, health, energy.

Action is our duty, victory our end; passivity and torpor are neither one nor the other; and if we could succeed in rendering ourselves impassive, that is to say, indifferent, sadness, which would deprive us of nothing, would, on the other hand, give us nothing either; it would pass uselessly over our heart, like those waves that continually lave the rocks they leave eternally sterile.

To suffer in vain is to frustrate God's plan; nay,

it is to make a tyrant of God. The moment that God afflicts me, and that grief leaves me as it found me, the pain, proceeding as it does from one stronger than I, becomes cruelty. You may in vain tell me that sorrow is common property, that no one escapes from it, that I could not, without utmost presumption, dream of an exceptional case made in my own favour; this coarse commonplace may indeed force itself upon my eyes, but it will never hinder them from weeping.

What! I alone of all the wounded and groaning creation to escape suffering! Do you think me mad enough to suppose it, selfish enough to wish it? Would I desire to be the only happy, to remain with a smile on my lips, while the rest of mankind were passing through the fire? But that others share my woes, that no one—not they more than I—can avoid the unavoidable; that we must needs endure, as we must needs die; that this state of things began with the beginning of the world, and is only to end with its close; this you might go on repeating to me for ever; it would never console me.

Neither would stoicism, even if I could attain to it, console me any better. In the eyes of many, it is good sense; in mine, it is mere folly.

I do not conceive that the soul has been created to be governed by events. To remain crushed

under the blow is not to make proof of im-
mortality.

You triumph, you tell me, because you come
paralysed out of the conflict, feeling nothing
further, neither pain nor joy; you are without
fear and without hope, an alien from other men,
indifferent to yourself, sublime to such a degree
that if your happiness depended upon drawing a
black ball or a white, you could put in your hand
into one or the other urn at random. And this,
some pretend, is wisdom; I hold it folly and
degradation. God has not invented this progress;
I conceive that such perfection offends him.
Sorrow that should lead straight to lethargy would
have missed its aim, disobeyed its mandate.

Then what is it that the God who afflicts me
demands? Prostrate, drowned in my tears, I do
not satisfy him. Dry, hard to my own sorrow,
careless as to my fate, I please him no better.
He forbids me rebellion; what then does he require, and why does he pursue after me thus?

Why? It is this *why*, this first cry of the soul,
this first question, overleaping the distance, that
God wants from us.

Why? Neither the acceptation of cowardice,
nor the compromise of philosophy, nor the delirium
of diversions, nor the languors of idleness, ask
why? This question, however audaciously it be

put, is a movement of the soul towards God. The tree that receives a stroke of the hatchet asks not why; the animal struck by a brutal hand goes howling to the skies, does not turn round, and ask its tyrant, Why; the ill-used child takes refuge in its mother's arms, it does not confront its persecutor with this why. But man offended walks straight to his brother man and puts the question; and the soul that God has smitten, if it lives, at one bound springs towards God, and says to God: Why?

There are many whys: The why of pride,—a protestation. He who utters it, at bottom cares not for further knowledge; he proclaims the injustice of God; he takes account of the cruelties of God; if God were to answer, he would not listen. God delights in tormenting men; his arrows pierce at random. What have I done to God? And this *why*, a defiance, a curse, echoes from bound to bound, down,—down into the depths of the abyss.

There is the why of frivolity, a noise that one makes in one's own ears, in order not to hear the message of the trial sent. This why goes knocking up there, down here, always out of reach, repeating a monotonous note, wearying the echoes, like, you would say, to one of those birds wandering in the woods, uneasy, astray, and all day long uttering the same note of complaint.

Then again, there is the why of inertia and self-indulgence. Hardly does it get itself shaped ; conscience tries to give it an impetus, but as soon as it rises it is cast down. From time to time a shock comes to stir it up ; it falls back. It is only good as a semblance of life, and a dispensation from action. If I knew why, I might try some expedient ; but I know not ; what then is to be done ?

There is also the why of despair. The heart, intoxicated with its woes, breathes out its hopelessness thus ; it is not a reproach, it is still less a prayer. The sufferer asks nothing, wants to know nothing ; what could men do—nay, what could God do in such a case as this ? One fact only is certain, irrevocable, my misery. Why ?—and the soul flies off, plunges into its anguish, and utters its cry at random. God might speak to it ; like one accused and called upon to justify his conduct, God might even explain to it the reasons of his dispensations ; this soul could not hear him ; it is too much absorbed in its affliction ; it can listen only to its sobs.

But here is a broken heart ; a poor heart that can endure no longer. Many thoughts stir within it, but they all trouble ; many voices address it, but not one has soothed. It no longer discerns

its way, the horizon is all dark ; one thing alone
it feels, and that is its suffering. Only it is a
simple heart, it knows that there is a God ; and in
all sincerity, and with that humility where breathes
the resolve of one great desire,—with that loyalty
that reveals the existence of an earnest will, it too
asks, Why? From that hour, between God and
that man, relations are established. Let be, he
will know why.

Why then? Before all, that we may know ourselves. On this head we were absolutely ignorant.
Suffering reveals self to us. Instead of that son of
God we had believed to be—lawful inheritor,
because never having dishonoured his father, or
denied his lofty lineage—we see appear a creature
equally mean and proud ; a union of incredible
presumption and inconceivable weakness ; an in-
grate full of unreasonable exactions ; a rebel who
heaps up all revolts, and claims all pardons ; one
indifferent to healthy delights, and enamoured of
sinful joys; an idolater of self; a sybarite who
makes others suffer without a scruple, and is killed
outright by an insect's sting ; a sinner who cares
nothing for heaven ; an impatient creature, exasperated by suspense ; a believer on smooth days,
a sceptic on rough; an undecided character, tossed
from good to evil, from ardour to torpor, from

action to idleness ; good for nothing, lost, unless, terrified at this self-encounter, he turns to God who is calling him, and makes up his mind to accept salvation.

It is well worth while, is it not, to buy, even **by** much suffering, this first response to our why?

But God has others in store for us.

In happiness we believe ourselves strong.   The navigator sailing over a quiet sea, easily persuades himself that he shall triumph over the hurricane. He is sure of himself; his bark is well built; the strong masts vibrate beneath the press of sail; look at the piercing eye and calm brow of the pilot ; the crew is a picked one ; anxiety is for others !   As for embarrassing one's-self with additional precautions, they are but cowards who do this.   Tempests, we defy you, and we put off !

Yes, but when that little cloud down there, thickening, spreading, shall have covered space ; when it shall have filled the sky with blackness ; when winds from I know not what quarter, unchained on all sides at once, shall furrow the humid plain ; when the water boils furious, mighty, opened up by invisible ploughshares, madly broken into foam ; when the winds howl ; when the waves give out a fatal roar; when strange hissing blasts tear away the sails as they pass by ; when the masts snap with a noise like thunder; when the heavy

seas fall upon the deck, and rush like cataracts
through the broken bulwarks,—then you will see
those foolhardy sailors with pale faces, growing
faint at the approach of death, cling frantically to
the spars and the rigging. Each wave breaks and
scatters ; one man disappears, then another, then
another. My beautiful bark, where are now thy
snowy sails, and thy proud flying flag ? Skill of
the pilot, courage of my crew, what has become
of you !

I did believe in God. He had given me all ;
and even though he should take back all, he would
have the right so to do, my broken heart would
not because of this become unbelieving. To
doubt the Father's love, to forget for a moment
all that Jesus himself suffered too, and that he has
the most precious grace for most extreme need ; to
become ungrateful because I am tried !—Never !

Warn others, if you will, of defection and revolt ;
bid them live by rule ; prescribe for them those
incessant prayers that exhaust the soul and weary
God ; I have no need of such. Prosperity has
found me stable, sorrow will not make me stumble
and fall. Suddenly some darling project fails ! I
know not what surprise pervades my spirit ; but how
ever, it is all very natural, and one must accept evil
as one has accepted good. An obstacle rears itself
in my path ; a prejudice defines itself more clearly,

a despotism threatens to be exerted, the heart is imprisoned, infidelities lacerate it, vices crush it, life grows impoverished, loneliness begins to make itself felt. I look for my faith; it was nigh at hand just now; I possessed it; by means of it, I called upon God, and he answered me; powers were given me; I used to rise to the higher region, and bring happiness thence; my submission, that Saviour whom I believed my brother, that energy that he was wont to bestow on me,—it is for these I am looking, and I can find no vestige of them. Rebellion that horrifies me begins to stir within, doubts come which put the last stroke to my desolation. Am I then so utterly poor and destitute? I cannot remain in such a state. I know what I will do : I will cry, entreat, obtain.

Blessed poverty! thou art the beginning of wealth.

We will not repeat what has been so often said, that it is the sorrows of earth that create the desire for heaven. God does not need the spoils of time to enrich his eternity. Just as he once transported an Enoch and an Elijah to the realms of light, without causing them to pass through the darkness of death, so now he can, without making our souls traverse the agonies of pain, kindle in them an ardent thirst for the happi-

ness to come. But the chariots of fire are not for
the many; the common road lies through the
grave; we reach the resurrection of the body, by
the dissolution of the body; we are taught to
aspire to eternal joys by the sorrows of the world.
An immeasurable distance stretches out between
God's paradise and these hearts of ours; scarcely
any but the despairing can prevail to overleap it.

The happy look at things on their own level,
the sorrowful look up; our thoughts settle where
our hope is fixed.

How full of rigorous truth and of ideal poetry
both, is that picture by Scheffer, of Jesus the Deliverer! Do you see those wan faces, those red-
dened eyelids? Those are the disappointed, the
ill-used of this life; they are seeking the day;
their raised arms stretch out towards the light. To
depart; that is what they are asking; to rise with
Jesus; to go where he is going; to be with him
for ever, in the full possession of an unfailing love.
Less sad, would they have been in such eager
haste? More laden with the enjoyments of earth,
would they have been equally resolute, equally
unchangeable in their decision?

I know not if you feel as I do; but hitherto in
these replies to our question *why*, I have only met
with myself, and this does not suffice me. nay, I

Q

might even say that this dries me up. Most certainly I desire to be saved,—it is the end of my existence ; lost myself, I should lose all ; my heart, that the divine wisdom purposes to renew, is moved to gratitude ; and yet, for all that, it remains sad, and asks whether, in order to prepare it for the skies, God had no gentler methods than these to employ ?

And now, look you, all at once I hear near me the voice of weeping ; I see beside me some dejected creature, laden with cares, exhausted by the toil that each morning renews, who lets his arms drop down, and sinks beneath his burden. If no one raises him, he will stay there on the ground. Then come passers by ; people of good health, prosperous circumstances, and great energy, cry to him : 'Look sharp ! Make an effort ! One must not give up thus ! When one is down, one gets up again.' Perhaps some vigorous hand will give him a shake in addition, or some iron arm will lift him up : 'There ! you are on your feet once more ; now walk.' He will try, poor miserable creature that he is, he will take a step or two, then sink down anew, and those flourishing persons I have described will turn away their heads in disgust at the cowardice and worthlessness of humanity.

Let them be indignant,—they may ; as for me, all bleeding myself, I can only sympathize. Each

groan of the poor sufferer reminds me of my own
sorrows, enters into my soul; it seems as though
I loved the one who wept thus. I approach, I
take his hand: 'Look at me, wilt thou? Thou
art suffering. I know the same suffering well;
thy energies are gone; I too have lost mine. If I
could help thee somewhat! Try to lean upon me;
thou wilt support me, I have need of pity; there
are hardly any but thou and I, bearing, as we do,
the same burden, who can understand each other.
Or else I will just come and sit me down beside
thee on the ground. I will not even speak to thee;
I will only look at thee; thine eyes will be able to
meet mine; it does good to weep, and when we
have wept we will pray. Thou wilt see—by and
by we shall slowly rise, shall go apart, take some
path unfrequented by those strong ones so ready
to treat rudely the weak.'

Indeed, the vigorous souls who have made a
place for themselves; the decided characters who
have established their rights; the lucid intellects
capable of lighting up all situations whatever,
would have great difficulty in even conceiving the
bondage of the weak. Each irresolution of their
fitful nature would cause more impatience than
compassion. Those stout-hearted ones would run a
great risk of wounding the feeble to death in their
very attempt to liberate them. The yoke that is

to be broken by a single blow, will very likely leave its splinters in the flesh; the irons that have to be burst by the pressure of a muscular hand, will, by their contraction, hurt and bruise the limbs they fetter. Let the slave draw near to the slave; let the one whom despotism is oppressing, speak to his oppressed brother; they will soon understand each other; they are acquainted with secrets for soothing servitude; the moment they have met, their condition becomes bearable. Perhaps they will find some means to escape; their mutual weakness will perhaps constitute an energy.

Or has destruction laid its hand on any man; does he wander in the midst of ruins, calling upon what is gone, cursing whatever is; crying 'Vanity, vanity' to all present joys? Is he seen, like the possessed of olden time, to dwell among the tombs, tearing his breast, and answering by cries of desolation all attempts made to console him? You—the happy ones—go away from this man, your very aspect exasperates him; your young faces, your eyes that have never wept, that pleasure you feel in mere existence, the enchantments of your illusions, nay, even your compassions—even that tenderly pitiful glance you cast upon him—all are felt as an insult. His misery is imbittered, his heart irritated by them all. But thou, for whom all the sweetnesses of love are over; thou, whom everything, even sorrow itself, has disappointed; thou, who hast seen thy affection, thy existence, thy own soul fail thee, come thou; put your despair together, open your hearts without a fear, no burst of joy will come to jar them. Your gloomy presence will spoil no happiness. Relate to each other how life deceived you; what word it was that, when everything crumbled away, Jesus sent you out of heaven; with tottering steps look out together for the rising road. Already you suffer less. Is it not so? It was a Brother that you were in need of.

If there are Christians free from weakness, let them pass us by on the other side. Their piety, which has never known a fall, makes us shiver. No passion has ever haunted them; they do not know the meaning of soul-torture. They walk straight forward, never faltering, stumbling, falling. What have such as they to say to us?

What! they would exclaim, you claim to belong to Christ, and you have divided hearts! What! envy, pride, enmities torture you! What means this battle-array? what all these uncertain proceedings? what is the use of such troubled consciences? People are only torn in two when they choose to be so. Cease your lamentation, martyrs of your own folly! The help your case needs is that of fire and sword. Nothing will raise you up but a stroke of the spur ; nothing will get you on but the lash.

Preserve us from contact with these perfect characters ! But if there be a Christian who knows the agony of conflict, who feels storms unloosed in his own heart ; if envy has corroded, doubts scorched, remorse gnawed him,—let him come ; he is one of us. Conqueror,—his success will teach us to war a good warfare ; overcome,—his reverses will inspire us with hope. Those others crushed us, their virtues blinded ; discouraged by their austerity, condemned by their justice, in their presence we could not even retain the energy to pray ; but this one does not dazzle me. He is one of my fellows ; where I fall he has faltered ; the hand that he reaches out to me trembles still ; it is his weakness gives him his strength ; stooping in the dust beside me, he lifts me in lifting himself ; we both stand once more, we retake our way ; we have good hope now ; yet a little time, and we shall arrive at home.

To console ! It is for this then that I have suffered ! What a light is shed, and how truly this, and this alone, is the balsam needed by my wounds ! My torn heart craved for a solace like this. Yes, it is true ; he who has not suffered will never be able to console. He may not lack the desire, indeed, but the sovereign science, the initiation, the revelation,—these he will ever lack. Jesus knew this ; he knew well that to be touched with our infirmities, he too must suffer as we do. It is thus that God raises me to himself.   By this ineffable power of consolation, by this truly heavenly privilege, God makes me a fellow-worker with him.

I, unworthy as I am ; I, so completely incapable ; what ! can I relieve the afflicted ? Will it do them good that I should share their trials ? Will that sad being regain hope, that unloving heart begin to love again, that man who could not pray clasp his hands in prayer; will the light of joy penetrate into that soul, and all this by means of some sorrows borne by me ? Oh, here I am, Lord ! Do thou only give me strength.   Behold, here I am !

Strength ! He who names strength names help.

It is a beautiful thing to console ; it is sublime to aspire to heaven ; it is very salutary to confess our sins; very valiant to labour at the regeneration of our soul; only we lack strength. I will be candid ; I will own that very often too we lack will as well.

If it were only to be morally transformed by the stroke of a wand, I would gladly consent to that. If God would only operate on me without co-

operation of mine, I should in no way resist him.
If he would introduce me, just as I am, into the
heavenly mansions, I should be enraptured.   But
the struggle frightens me ; and what appals me
most of all is that tremendous effort requisite to
give myself away.   There are moments when I
would fain possess my God.   Earth vanishes then ;
he alone endures.   But at other times it is God
that disappears, and it is the world that takes hold of
me.   Where shall I grasp myself, so as to lead myself
captive to my king ? Who will lay his sceptre on
the legions of my thoughts, and subject them ?
How shall I make my heart *will ?*   My reason, so
clear in speech, so weak in action, may indeed
silence that heart, but can never change it.

Such a state as this cannot last.   It is impossible
that God who has measured out the space between
heaven and earth, and who says to man, ' Come up
hither,' should not, at the same time, let fall some
golden cable that man may cling to.   Strength will
indeed be required to seize hold of it; without
persistence on our part, the cable would escape ;
but the cable does exist ; if it did not, God would
not be God.

I feel the approach of one that is mighty ; one
that is invincible is drawing towards me.   My eyes
have not discerned him ; nevertheless he is there.
No sound has struck upon my ear; but for all that,

I hear him. He exerts no constraint, but I go forth to meet him. He has not overthrown me, but I feel as though I belonged to him. I may indeed grieve him, and then he retires; but in this liberty to dispense with him which he leaves me, I feel myself more than ever a slave, the slave of evil. If I call him, he returns; if I hold him fast, he abides; if I show him my sub- jugated soul, he infuses energy therein, he imparts to me a vehemence which makes me an athlete and a conqueror. When I take my undecided, congealed heart in my two hands, as it were, and cry out, 'All is over; it is dead, nothing can be done with it any more;' he does not so readily despair. Like an eagle warming her young beneath her wings, he transmits the spark of life. My heart rekindles; it is love alone that can inspire love.

What weakness checks me, what fear silences? What! do I not dare then to speak the Holy Spirit's name! Without his tenderness, I should perish. When I had forsaken my God, forgotten Jesus, when I was flying far away on the wrong road, when prayer had died upon my lips, when sin was victorious in every contest,—he thought upon me—me, the wicked, the mean; he followed after me, he found me, he asked me what ailed me that I walked on thus, a wild, hardened, un- happy creature! He did not begin by reproaches;

he listened to my complaint; he let me say all that was in my heart. Very gently he drew me on in the direction of the Father; while still far off, he showed me that Father with arms opened wide to receive me; it was thanks to him, that I began to desire conversion; he regenerated my will, he restored rectitude to my conscience, and shall I now be ashamed of confessing him? Because he is little spoken of, shall I not speak of him? Because his communion has I know not what reputation of being mystical; because quietism has laid claim to his name, distorted his character, calumniated his influence; because the wise of this world smile at the folly of a spirit which is not the spirit of man; because it may be said of him, as once it was said of Jesus, ' Have any of the rulers believed on him?' —shall I then fail to acknowledge him; nay, shall I betray?

Just now we were treating of consolation; who has ever consoled like the Holy Spirit?

There may be situations when an angel's word would bruise the heart. He,—he does not articulate a single word; he only pours drop by drop the divine oil upon the wound, and the wound closes.

Bereavement has reached us; the Holy Spirit transports us into heavenly places; he restores to us our dead.

The wrath of God threatened through our trials;

the Holy Spirit brings the tender mercies of God within our reach. Jesus, seated at the right hand of the Father, did no doubt walk once upon this earth, but he walks here no more; the Holy Spirit brings back Jesus from heaven. Yes, it is indeed the Saviour; we have caught the hem of his garment. The Holy Spirit says to me, Pray; I do pray. But he does more; he takes my trembling prayer, he offers it to God, it is accepted of him. When I read the Scriptures, thanks be to the Holy Spirit, they are no longer mere words; they are the very voice of my Master; they live; they give me life. Without the Holy Spirit, should I burn with the desire to wipe away tears; should I bend beneath the weight of sufferings not my own, and that aggravate my woes; should I be found uneasy about other souls; should I not leave to perish those who are bent upon perishing? This I can no longer do. As the Holy Spirit loves, so I love also. As he prays, I pray. As he is moved with burning and unutterable desire, so I am moved. I am a new man; I have recovered my soul. I no longer weep as one despairing, or rebellious, or cowardly; even sorrow has acknowledged its master.

Is it not so? Our hearts burn within us. Thus the disciples of Emmaus were vaguely conscious of the presence of Jesus. He will abide with us, —he, and not another. Our eyes begin to discern him; it is his gentle voice speaks to us those oft-repeated words, ' It is I, be not afraid.'

We might indeed be afraid of God. So long as Jesus has not folded us in his love, the awful holiness of God rises before us, and we are terrified.

We are afraid too of men. Man who has not made the heart, exacts everything, gives little, often understands nothing. But afraid of Jesus! It is not possible! I find this blessedness in him, that he is thoroughly acquainted with me. He has created me; he knows where I am vulnerable; my impotence does not irritate him; he has fixed my limitations. He may indeed see me faithless; but he does not lose hope of me, for he sees me repentant. Because I am cast down, he does not give me up for lost. If I am tempted, he was not ignorant of Satan's devices, and knew too that my poor heart would probably be misled by them. Jesus has the measure of my strength; what I can do, he will have me to do, but he requires nothing beyond.

But I need still more than this.

There are fathers who keep their sons at a distance. The son knows that he is beloved, but for all that, a certain deference fetters him; ceremony presides over their mutual relations; he would not tell everything whatever to his father. And if that son has depressed spirits, above all, if he be self-dissatisfied, respectful to the degree of constraint, naturally reserved, he will keep his own counsel ; he will learn to suffer alone, and being alone, perhaps he will fall.   My Saviour is not such a father ; he is not a formal friend, into whose house there is no entering except in full dress. Such as I am, I go ; it signifies little when ; the worse my state, the greater my claim upon Jesus.   Before all, he belongs to those who have need of him.

Lay bare your real heart to your best earthly friend, and you will detect some alarm in his eyes. Just try to drop in at odd hours at one of your intimates ; go to him when you are tired, morose, ill-tempered ; ask him for his time, his money, for what he has and what he has not ; he will take you for a madman. Pour out on a poor human creature the sum of your sorrows, in their detail as well as in their aggregate ; spare him none of your retrospections, inconsistencies, ardours ; throw before him your sins, what they have been, what they are ; the feelings that glow beneath the ashes, the thoughts that scathe your soul, your fevered passions, the inextricable complication of your conflicting impulses,—you would appal him, and you would kill him. Pity for those we love, to say nothing of the confusion of face our own wretchedness inspires, will for ever place a restraint upon our lips. Always the fear of wearying affection, the terror of destroying it, the shame of what we are, will keep closed the sluices of the heart.

And yet a suffering that one owns loses its sting; the sorrow that we have to hide gnaws the heart like the gangrene. It is so good to be one's-self, one's own whole self undisguised. With Jesus, I am this. I have upon him the claim that lepers had. They had no scruple in stopping him on his way; Jesus used to touch them, and they were healed. So with me; Jesus lays his hand on me, and heals me too.

And as he knows our nature which he has made, so too he knows our griefs which he has endured.

When the rich man approaches the poor to compassionate the sadness of his indigent lot, the poor fixes upon the rich a sceptical gaze. That rich man has relieved him; for this he is grateful. But as to sympathy, how believe in that? can one understand what one has never felt? Now Jesus has felt all. The sick man whom He visits will not shake his head when spoken to of patience; Jesus will not meet that bitter, almost ironical smile with which, in gloomy silence, the man who suffers receives the consolations of the man who has never known suffering.

Poor! Jesus was poor! Depreciated! Who

was ever more so? He who came eating and
drinking, public respectability was in arms against
him. He, the disturber of the people, the destroyer of the law—why, Caiaphas listening to his
words, tore his robes, and cried out, Blasphemy!
He, the pretender to the throne of Israel, dragged
by the partisans of order and good government
before Pilate, condemned by Pilate to be beaten
with rods, and crowned with thorns. Oppressed!
Jesus lived in the very midst of the coarse and
ignorant, and those rough natures weighed upon
him. Weary! No cross in the world could ever
repeat his lassitudes. Despoiled in his affections!
Judas sells him; Peter denies; his brothers even
proclaim him mad. Tortured by inner conflicts!
Satan tempted him. Moved with beautiful sadness! Ah, yes! Beyond doubt he sighed for the
kingdom of truth; he yearned to save the world;
his exile from heaven caused him all the languor
of an immense desire. Afraid of death; trembling
at the thought of encountering the divine justice!
the agony of Gethsemane answers to ours.

Confident, therefore, that He knows all that I
can suffer, I open out my heart to him with an
absolute trust. Neither the cruel ignorance which
has so often wounded me, nor the awkwardness
of a kind heart untaught by the sorrows of life,
nor the exactions of a hard nature that the diffi-

culties of the way have never softened; none, in short, of those arrows that our inexperience sends deep into the flesh of our fellow-creatures, will ever assail me from him.

But what makes me so tedious a creature is that I am so weak a one. Smitten by the same blows, I go on repeating the same cries. I tell and re-tell my afflictions, I weary with these even the kindest ears. People may indeed love me, but they find the monotony of my tears very hard to endure. The friendship that could resist my faults, gets worn out by my lamentations. If indeed it could do me any good, it would undertake a far severer ordeal; but it cannot, and therefore the uniformity of my wail oppresses it, because it keeps it motionless in presence of its own incapacity. Love feels itself giving way before the irrevocable. Our feelings can no more maintain their life in a state of complete impotence than a flame can burn in a vacuum. So long as a friend can soothe us he willingly listens; the good he is doing stimulates his compassion. If his sympathy grows useless; if he finds us every morning just as he leaves us every night, his strength deserts him. The spring is exhausted; our thirst has dried it up without quenching itself. Now Jesus is all-powerful; and this is one of the secrets of his boundless patience. He who applies to him, were it for the thousandth time, will always return consoled. It is not to the unhappy that Jesus forbids 'repetitions;' he knows that our sobs are not 'vain;' the heart that heaves them lives, and gives itself in them. Has not he himself related to us the widow's importunity; has he not said, Do likewise?

I do so, O my God. Importunate without fear; I come, I will come again. I tell all; I will tell again. What else indeed is prayer than this?

I have a confession to make : I believe in the power of prayer; I believe that God takes an interest in the small affairs of the small creatures that he has placed upon this small globe. I have a conviction that each murmur of our trembling voices, sometimes stifled with tears, is distinguished by God amidst the harmonies, perhaps the sobs of the universe. I believe that when it is good for us, God grants our petitions.

You wish to know how I reconcile the partial accident of the realization of our prayers with the immutable order of God's decrees? I do not reconcile it.

I live upon a grain of dust; God reigns in heaven. I can hardly distinguish one atom from another; God embraces the immensity of past, present, future. Now this God has said to me; Ask all, I will give all. I hear and I obey.

If you press me hard, I shall venture to remind you of the divine prescience which knew the prayers I should one day utter before I myself had seen the light. That which God has known beforehand he may have heeded beforehand.

You insist! Then I in my turn will put a question to you : Are you not absolutely free to speak, to think, and, within certain limits, to do what you like? Nevertheless, your acts, words, thoughts, which create events, are included in the eternal order. How do you reconcile the liberty that you have and that you exercise, with the immutable organization of things?

In the night of my own ignorance I grasp the words of my God, I walk in their light. They do not reveal everything, but they never deceive.

'Ah, I understand!' people say ; 'you solicit the salvation of your soul from God ; you commend to him the spiritual interests of humanity.'

I ask everything from him.

'What, you concern yourself about the troubles of this life, you lay stress upon its ephemeral joys?'

I do.

'You have the presumption to imagine that God above will take the trouble to gratify you ; that your affairs occupy him ; that he grants at one

and the same time myriads of conflicting petitions ?'

I have a limited mind, as I have told you ; I
do not seek to go beyond God's teaching. What
he gives me I take ; I do not inquire into what he
has withheld. If there are difficulties, if there are
mysteries—impossibilities, if you will—God is well
able to dispose of them without any interference
of mine.

Jesus has commanded me to open my heart
and to stretch out my hands ; it is enough for me
to do as Jesus tells me. The apostles implored
from God the recovery of a friend ; when they
were in prison, they asked to get out of it ; when
they were persecuted, beaten, they cried to Him
for help ; and yet they were well aware that afflic-
tións await us, that our sorrows enter into the
divine plan ; but submissive and persevering at the
same time, they prayed to God to deliver them,
and God did deliver.

What was it that Jesus did when the bloody
sweat rolled from his face, and with his broken
voice he went on repeating : Father, must I drink
this cup ? Father, if it were possible, remove this
cup from me !

You will tell me that even then the will of Jesus
bowed before the will of the Father. And do you
suppose that mine resists him ? Is the being con-

fiding a symptom of rebellion? Ah, be very sure no lips more sincerely cry, 'Thy will be done,' than lips accustomed to ask for everything. The child who is used to no reticences, whose heart has neither secrets nor false shame; he who runs to his father and now asks bread, now leans upon his breast to implore pardon,—that child will have learnt obedience, his father's kindness will have taught it to him. But the shy and taciturn son; he who alike keeps to himself his wishes and his sorrows; timid because he loves little; distrustful because he does not believe in love; who only approaches his father on great occasions; this son will resent a refusal; he knows little of his father's tenderness, and therefore his severities wound him.

'Such details tend to lower God.'

For whom then do you take God? You make him altogether such a one as ourselves; you attribute to him human proportions.

God, it is written, humbleth himself to behold the things that are in heaven and earth. As much to search out the limitless height and depth of the skies as to consider this poor little globe that rolls along, amidst the starry myriads. The fall of empires, the arcana of politics, are as small in the eyes of God as the trouble of some poor perplexed and afflicted heart. I am wrong; it is the heart that is great; sorrow that is of importance. The anxieties of a mother have weight in the Divine balance. And if the fate of nations did not involve human destinies ; if it were not interwoven with those individual joys and woes which you think so trifling ; if these existences that you hold so cheap were not affected thereby, do you suppose that God would heed it ?

A God confined to the infinitely great is a God infinitely limited ; your God who only occupies himself with weighty matters ; that overtasked God who abandons the care of everyday interests to inferior agents ; the God who gives his signature as it were unconcernedly from afar, just as a hard-worked minister of state remits the rubbish of un-important documents to his clerks,—that God is but a mutilated, impotent idol, the paltry creation of man's own feeble intellect. I know and I adore the Infinite God, infinite goodness, infinite love ; the God for whom everything is little and every-thing is great ; the God in whose sight a soul is of more value than a world ; the God who takes count of the tears of children ; the God who has said to me, Ask and thou shalt receive. That is my God. I know not any other.

Will you hear another astonishing fact? I speak to this God at every hour of the day. That com-mand, Pray without ceasing, which scares so many people, constitutes my safety and makes my happiness. It is not enough for me to think about God, my soul must pour itself out before him.

When you have some beloved being beside you, does it suffice you to think of him? Not to speak to him,—why, would not that be a torture? Every time an idea occurs to you, a feeling overflows, you speak! Ah! if the fear of wearying did not restrain us, how far more freely would our heart give itself expression!

One can never weary God.

What is it I say to him? What does one say to one's father; and to one's mother what does one not say? Is any eloquence required? All fear over, embarrassment gone, the lips move as the heart prompts, and the mother is satisfied, the father rejoiced.

But I have to go still further, and give fresh offence. I am one of those who read the Bible.

The Bible! as well give one's-self out a Puritan at once ;—the most displeasing personage that the world ever saw. Prayer may indeed pass; for though philosophy smiles at it, elegance can tolerate it still. But the Bible! The book of the Calvinist, the formulary of all that is stiff, the sum of all that is narrow! Who can hear the Bible spoken of without conjuring up the angular profile of a preacher,—with spectacles on nose, thin lips, dull glance, sour voice, pedantic manner, awkward gesture? He does not speak, he emits sentences; he has only one idea, to convert his neighbour by Bible blows; his heart is regulated like a chronometer, wound up every four-and-twenty hours; his character, moulded upon mean and gloomy ordinances, has lost all individuality; he never laughs; seldom allows himself tears; if automatons had souls, his would be the soul of an automaton, acting by rule, moving mechanically; placing itself in opposition to life, like those great stones against which torrents fret, which stir not, roll not, impassive and inert.

Well then, I love with all the strength of my soul this Bible that it is so unfashionable to be acquainted with. Did I not love it, there would be no words to qualify my insensibility; were I to hesitate to declare my love, my mean cowardice would exceed my ingratitude. When happy, I grasp the book that God has given me; my happiness is not disturbed thereby; rather my joys are intensified by finding there limitless horizons. If unhappy, teased by cares, shaken in my faith, rebellious, famishing for truth, oh, how well it comforts me, this word of my God! It is pure as rock crystal, more radiant than the sun, and it is human as well. It opens the heaven of heavens, and it comes down to illuminate the most obscure corners

of the poorest lives. It issues from the heart of
God, and it makes itself a home in my heart, such
as it is. It conveys the thoughts of God, and
speaks to me mouth to mouth. I come to it all
bruised and bleeding; I have been repulsed; the
best have hurt me by their touch; sometimes they
are severe and exact too much; sometimes they
weakly leave me to sink in my languor. Not so
the Bible; it has savour that refreshes me, gentleness that soothes my sorrows; it rekindles the little
faith about to die, it is an earnest of God's faithful-
ness, a witness of his love for me. Through it, I
know that Jesus wept; it assures me that I am
his and that he is mine; it is the voice, the very
voice of my heavenly Father. No other has ever
spoken to me as it has done.

Oh yes, I am quite aware that lofty intellects
look down upon us with pity. Great minds have
found out, for the thousandth time since the Bible
has existed, that it is but a tissue of error. I continue, however, to be misled, and I will confess to
you that these terrible attacks, while they afflict my
heart, leave my soul perfectly undisturbed. Here
are now eighteen centuries that the wisdom of this
world has been overthrowing the Scriptures; for
all that, the Scripture has lost neither jot nor tittle.
Go, ask the dying if its lamp that lights up the
passage of death has grown paler; ask the bereaved,

if its promises no longer uphold; ask the sinner who detests his pollution, and would fain find out heaven, if the Bible has ceased to show him the way! Each generation of presumptuous men buffets it in turn, with what shouts of derision we all know; but while generations fall one after the other into dust, the Bible continues to save souls, to regenerate lives, and to console hearts. Laugh on if you will! The Bible has the gentleness of eternal things; it has seen pass your fathers, it will see you pass.

We who believe, we have very often dreamed of those primitive ages, when the tent of the patriarchs reared itself in the plains of Judea. Then an Abraham would come forth from it, would go and walk beneath the terebinth trees, and God would speak with him. Our hearts have leaped within us; we have cried out, Oh, if God still spoke to man, how he would tell me all I want to hear!

I assure you that God speaks still.

Listen. There are the Psalms. You have heaved these very sighs; this horror of yourself, you too have experienced it. These doubts of the truth, this dread of the grave, this ignorance of God's ways, this insane condemning of his acts, all this is indeed yours. Here, now, are hymns of triumph. Faith has returned, grace is once more possessed, joy descends in floods this is equally familiar to you, and this is of God. It is the eternal encounter of the heart of man with the heart of the Father. Always light will break forth, always joys will spring from such a contact as this.

If any one came and said to you, Jesus is about to pass by, at a bound you would leave everything whatever. You would be seen mingled with the crowd, following the Master, and when you were obliged to return, your eyes would have a different look. Jesus does pass by still ; the Gospels restore him to us. He fixes his gaze upon you, his hand touches you ; he addresses to you one of those words which sink to the very heart's core ; never before had he uttered them in a tone so tender, so penetrating, and it is to you individually that he speaks.

But here we have need of patience.

We do not know how to wait. We are like children who stamp at the least delay. Our wills have in the ardour of their exactions all that they want in earnestness and persistency. As soon as he is kept in suspense, the child loses all zest for his toy. It is by his slowness in answering us that God would transform our wishes into purposes. Patient expectation is a sign of spiritual vitality. He who knows not how to wait, is not worthy to obtain.

If, on the contrary, we do not meet with God

at the first few steps we take towards him, all is
over! there is no God! If revelatior opposes
some obscurities ; if we imagine that we have discovered in it some contradictions ; if hard work,
and steeping the soil with the sweat of our brow
in order to find the gold, be needed, we pronounce
that there is no gold to be found. The Bible
has nothing to give us ; it is but one lie more, a
final deception. Because Jesus, who has, it may
be, called us all our lives long unheeded, does
not hasten to us the very first moment that our
lips have tried to stammer out his name ; because
he strengthens, by letting it grow up in silence,
the need. we begin to feel of him,—Jesus aban- ·
dons us, he closes his ears, our cries are vain !
And yet we know very well how to wait for the
success of our enterprises here below. Let some
man in power hold our future in suspense, we
are patient, we persevere ; dumb, if need be, but
decided, come what may, never to relax our hold.
It is this tenacity that God requires from us.
The happiness he has to bestow is well worth it.

And now, would it be too great a descent to
look a little at this earth of ours ?

For earth too has her consolations. A fine day
seems but a small thing, but what eloquence these
tender mercies of the sky have for my heart !

Do what you will with the country ; beautiful or not, it is still the work of God.

To walk with the breeze upon one's brow, to trample the level grass exuberant with freshness, to climb upon the mountain, to follow through the meadows some thread of water gliding under rushes and water-plants,—I give you my word for it, there is happiness in this. At this contact with healthy and natural things, the follies of the world drop off as drop the dead leaves when the spring sap rises, and the young leaves put forth. The pangs of the heart lose their vehemence. The great blue sky which reflects itself in the soul gives it its own peace. The divine goodness, pity, and power wrap us round ; it is a halt, as it were, upon the threshold of paradise.

This morning my head is heavy, my heart restless ; I go out into the fields. Here is the border of the wood ; there are wild geraniums here ; thin bunches of lilac flowers trail to the foot of the tall trees ; here, close at hand, are poppies bending beneath the breeze, and clouding the corn-fields with red waves : there, orchids display their velvet dress in the shade. Who can tell the charm of the great silence, the silence of these out-of-the-way spots ! Myriads of birds and insects traverse the air, a freshness floats beneath the tree-tops, the solitude is absolute. I have seen all this before ; to-day it seems more beautiful than ever. I bury my face in grass that no foot has ever trodden; I fling all my cares into it. It does one good to think of nothing, just to open out one's heart to the sun. The pines thrill above my head, and when I look up I see the clear sky beyond their highest branches. The aromatic atmosphere invigorates my soul. Here things assume their proper places. It is the temple of the Lord; I find light here that is not met with elsewhere. And then I wander on at random; I gather whatever comes under my hand. These sheaves of wild-flowers freely mown make holiday in my heart. Reflection! analysis! I leave that to others; I feel that God is good, and I want nothing further.

Or else on one of those October days which rise all radiant after they have once shaken off their mantle of mist, let us take our way into lonely places. The brambles are reddening on the mountains, we hear the lowing of the herds shaking their bells in the pastures. Here and there some fire rolls out its smoke; insects rise slowly with their little balloons of white silk; the bushes, deceived by the mildness of the nights, put forth fresh shoots; the great daisies, the scarlet pinks, the sage-plants that had flowered in June, open out a few bright petals here and there. This will not last : winter is coming on. What of that?

This last smile tells me that God loves and means to console me.

If you but knew what delight it gives just to stir about the earth ; yes, to plant, to prune, to work in the open air, to eat with appetite a good piece of dry bread ! If you knew how many griefs this spade cuts down at the roots, and what vexations one buries under these clods turned over ! You have no garden ? Still a bit of sky remains to you, a window, something or other. Put down creepers there—mignonette—anything you like ; let that grow, let it have green leaves ; you are no longer quite so unhappy ; you are taken out of yourself. You too can quench your thirst at pure fountains ; the gladness of nature has overflowed on you.

I know other aids besides.

Have you ever given pleasure to any one ? If so, you know what happiness is.

However bereaved and dispirited existence may have left me, sorrowful unto death ; still if I can bring back a smile on those withered lips ; if that little child, seeing me arrive, jumps with joy ; if some fair dream, suddenly realized by my means, bursts in upon a life long destitute of joy ; if thou, my God, dost deign to make use of thy poorest creature to gladden one of the disinherited ones of this world,—I feel a reflex of paradise illuminate my heart. A benign constellation has risen in my sky ; my griefs have lost their bitterness, my courage has returned ; nay, I even find some sweetness in life. So long as God sees fit to leave me on earth, I will walk in it with a cheerful heart.

You love' no one ! Try, I entreat you ; it is not so difficult to love some one.

The people who surround you are, you say, so disagreeable ! Who knows, the least attractive may perhaps become to you the most dear. Everybody knows them, those last comers, those poor youngest children that make their appearance unexpectedly ; one burden the more, another mouth to feed ; and the mother's health was not good, and the father is getting old. They are endured, and that is all. Wait awhile ; the one child too many will prove the star lit in the midnight. Why is it that the brothers are in such a hurry to leave their work ? A cradle awaits them, little hands that clap with impatience at their approach. What is it that has restored vigour to the father ? Do you hear him, how briskly he is chopping away, and singing the while ? He is thinking of the child too many. This evening he will see him, take him in his arms, kiss him. He is getting on well, the little rogue ; he'll make a man some of these days ! And the mother, the poor mother that the first wail of this child so pained, only ask her whether she would like to be without him ; this soft, toddling thing, with arms held out to her the whole day through.

And then again let us work ; believe me, this is the great essential. The inert contemplation of our troubles exercises an unwholesome fascination over our nature. A serpent lurks there with poison beneath its fang.

Work which snatches us away from ourselves, frees our heart from the mean selfishness of life. Effort, by calling out our energies, makes men of us. He who constrains his mind to toil, knows little of the torpors of sadness. Temptations to rebellion seldom triumph, except over debilitated hearts ; the idle soul bows beneath the tyranny of vanity ; the sufferings of the mind belong to emptiness of mind ; the doleful creatures to the waste places ; the heavy days are the listless days. Show me an unoccupied person ; I am bold to pronounce that he is unhappy.

If you have a voice, if you can hold a brush, if colours obey you, if melodies sing themselves to your ear, thank God ! he has given you the golden key. The delights of the ideal world will shed their lustre round you. For an hour at least you will rise to the spheres of g'ory ; the conceits of angels will

ravish you. Crushed beneath the vulgarities of
the world, a nobleness will be yours. Dejected,
oppressed, disappointed, tones of lofty poetry will
recite to you your sadness. It will seem to you as
though tears answered to your tears. The cup
filled with ambrósia has come in contact with your
lips, and having tasted it you rise more strong.

We must part. My heart contracts. You who
suffer, you were there, methought; our tears had
mingled; I felt the pressure of your hand.

Is it over, then? Shall we meet each other no
more? Oh, yes. I hear you still; you are not far
from me. We pray, do we not? We implore hope
to support our sorrows; we desire energy to carry
on our struggle. Soon the eternal day will dawn;
then we, the sad, whom Jesus has consoled, the
poor sinners whom Jesus has raised, we shall easily
recognise each other's faces. 'This one,' we shall
say, 'is my brother. In the great tribulation I
met with him, and I loved him.'

CARTERS' FIRESIDE LIBRARY.

FIRST SERIES.—75 Cents each.

By A. L. O. E.

The Claremont Tales.	The Chief's Daughter.
The Adopted Son.	Shepherd of Bethlehem.
The Young Pilgrim.	The Lost Jewel.
Giant-Killer, and Sequel.	Stories on the Parables.
Flora; or, Self-Deception.	Ned Manton.
The Needle and the Rat.	War and Peace.
Eddie Ellerslie, and the Mine	The Robber's Cave.
Precepts in Practice.	The Crown of Success.
The Christian's Mirror.	Rebel Reclaimed.
Idols in the Heart.	The Silver Casket.
Pride and His Prisoners.	Christian Conquests.
The Poacher.	Try Again.

Anna ; or, Passages from the Life of a Daughter at Home.
Aunt Edith ; or, Love to God the Best Motive.
Mabel Grant: a Highland Story.
Memoir of Captain W. T. Bate of the Royal Navy.
St. Augustine.   By the REV. JOHN BAILLIE.
The Black Ship: with other Allegories and Parables.
Blind Lilias.   With Introd. by REV. C. B. TAYLER.
Blind Man's Holiday : or, Short Tales for the Nursery.
Blossoms of Childhood.
The Indian Tribes of Guiana.   By BRETT.
Broad Shadows on Life's Pathway.
The Brother and Sister ; or, the Way of Peace.
The Brother's Watchword.
The Pilgrim's Progress.   By JOHN BUNYAN.
Clara Stanley ; or, A Summer among the Hills.
Little Crowns and How to Win Them.   By COLLIER.
The Cottage and Its Visitor.

Day-Break; or, Right Struggling and Triumphant.
Days at Muirhead; or, Little Olive's Holidays.
Days of Old: Three Stories from Old English History.
Emily Vernon. By Mrs. DRUMMOND.
Children of the Manse. By Mrs. DUNCAN.
Tales of the Scottish Peasantry.
Edward Clifford; or, Memories of Childhood.
Ellie Randolph; or, The Good Part.
Fanny Aiken: A Story for Girls.
Far Off; or, Asia and Australia Described.
Florence Egerton; or, Sunshine and Shadow.
Vesper: A Series of Tales. By the COUNTESS DE GASPARIN.
Alice and Adolphus. By Mrs. GATTY.
Aunt Judy's Tales.   "   "
Parables from Nature.   "   "
May Dundas; or, Passages from Young Life.
Grandma's Sunshine: A Series of Stories.
The Happy Home. By the Rev. J. HAMILTON, D. D.
Memoir of Lady Colquhoun. By Dr. HAMILTON.
Haste to the Rescue. By Mrs. WIGHTMAN.
Life of General Havelock. By BROCK.
The Infant's Progress. By Mrs. SHERWOOD.
Jamie Gordon; or, The Orphan.
Jeanie Morrison; or, the Discipline of Life.
The Earnest Christian; a Memoir of Mrs. Jukes.
Kate Kilborn, or, Sowing and Reaping.
Kate and Effie; or, Prevarication.
Kitty's Victory, and Other Stories.
Life of Richard Knill of St. Petersburg.
The Lighted Valley.—Memoir of Abby Bolton.
Little Lychetts. By the Author of " John Halifax."
Louis and Frank.
The Family at Heatherdale. By Mrs. MACKAY.
Mabel's Experience; or, Seeking and Finding.

Margaret Warner; or, The Young Wife at the Farm.
Maud Summers the Sightless.
The Convent. By Mrs. McCRINDELL.
Mia and Charlie; or, A Holiday at Rydale Rectory.
Ministering Children · a Tale. 2 vols. 18 Engravings.
School-Days and Companions.
Near Home; or, The Countries of Europe Described. ◆
Best Things. By the Rev. RICHARD NEWTON, D. D.
King's Highway. By Rev. Dr. NEWTON.
The World of Waters. By Mrs. OSBORNE.
Passing Clouds; or, Love Conquering Evil.
Tales of the Covenanters. By POLLOK.
The Rival Kings. By the Author of "Sidney Grey."
Round the Fire: a Series of Stories.
Ruth and Her Friends: a Story for Girls.
The Sale of Crummie: a Scotch Story.
Sydney Grey: a Tale of School Life.
Olive Leaves. By Mrs. SIGOURNEY.
Letters to my Pupils.   '
Water-Drops.   "
Holiday House: a Series of Tales. By SINCLAIR.
Roughing It with Alick Baillie. By STEWART.
Tales of English History.
Tales of Sweden and the Norsemen.
Tales of Travellers. By MARIA HACK.
The Contributions of Q. Q. By JANE TAYLOR.
Tony Starr's Legacy; or, Faith in a Covenant God.
The Torn Bible.
Abbeokuta; or, Sunrise in the Tropics. By TUCKER.
The Rainbow in the North.   "
Southern Cross and Southern Crown.   "
Warfare and Work; or, Life's Progress.
The Way Home.
The Week. By author of " Commandment with Promise."
Willie and Unica.

Life of William Wilberforce.
Wilson's Lights and Shadows of Scottish Life.
Win and Wear: a Story for Boys.
Woodcutter of Lebanon and Exiles of Lucerna.

SECOND SERIES.—65 Cents each.

Africa's Mountain Valley.
Ashton Cottage; or, The True Faith: a Tale.
Life Studies. By Rev. John BAILLIE.
Bertie Lee; or, A Father's Prayers Answered.
Brook Farm; or, American Country Life.
Charles Roussell; or, Industry and Honesty.
The Children on the Plains. By AUNT FRIENDLY.
The Commandment with Promise: a Story.
Cosmo's Visit to His Grandfather.
The Cottage Fireside. By the Rev. Dr. DUNCAN.
First and Last Journey; the Story of Rhoda Williams.
Frank Netherton; or, The Talisman.
Fritz Harold; or, The Temptation.
The Jewish Twins. By AUNT FRIENDLY
Johnson's Rasselas.
The Last Week. By DAVIS JOHNSON, JR.
Magdala and Bethany. By the Rev. S. C. MALAN.
Marion's Sundays; or, Stories on the Commandments.
Michael Kemp, the Happy Farmer's Lad.
The Mine; or, Darkness and Light. By A. L. O. E.
New Cobwebs to Catch Little Flies.
The Giants and How to Fight Them. By Dr. NEWTON.
Opie's Tales about Lying.
The Last Shilling. By Rev. P. B. POWER.
The Three Cripples.   "   "
The Two Brothers.   "   "
Annals of the Poor. By LEGH RICHMOND.

The Boy's Book. By Mrs. SIGOURNEY.
The Girl's Book. "
Original Poems. By JANE TAYLOR.
Life of Captain Hedley Vicars, 97th Regiment.

THIRD SERIES.—50 Cents each.

Annie Price: a Series of Stories.
The Three Bags of Gold. By A. L. O. E.
Beautiful Home. By the Author of " Minis. Children."
The Black Cliff. By A. L. O. E.
The Broken Chain. "
The Buried Bible and Other Stories.
Esther Parsons. By A. L. O. E.
The Farmer's Daughter. By Mrs. CAMERON.
The Cities of Refuge. By MACDUFF.
Diamond Brooch and Other Stories.
The Faithful Sister.
Falsely Accused. By A. L. O. E.
Fanny, the Flower-Girl; or, Honesty Rewarded.
Frank Harrison.
The Circle of Blessing. By Mrs. GATTY.
Motes in the Sunbeam. "
Proverbs Illustrated, "
Worlds Not Realized. "
The Giant Killer. By A. L. O. E.
The Great Journey; an Allegory. By MACDUFF.
The Lake of Galilee. By Dr. HAMILTON.
Harry Dangerfield. By A. L. O. E.
Anna Ross: a Story for Children. By GRACE KENNEDY.
Profession Is Not Principle. "
Philip Colville: a Covenanter Story. "
Father Clement: a Roman Catholic Story. "
Little Willie. By the Author of " Round the Fire."
The Lost Spectacles.

The Gold Thréad. By NORMAN MACLEOD, D. D.
Morning. A Book for Mothers and Children.
Mother's Last Words and other Ballads.
My Neighbour's Shoes, or Feeling for Others. By A.L·O.E.
My School-Boy Days.
My Youthful Companions.
Old Friends with New Faces. By A. L. O. E.
Old Margie's Flower Stall.
Parliament in the Play-Room. By A. L. O. E.
Paying Dear for It.   "
The Rambles of a Rat.   "
A Ray of Light to Brighten Cottage Homes.
The Roby Family. By A. L. O. E.
Charlie Seymour ; or, The Good Aunt and the Bad Aunt.
Stories on the Lord's Prayer.
Stories of Jewish History. By A. L. O. E.
Stories of the Ocean. By the Rev. JOHN SPAULDING.
Three Months Under the Snow.
Display: a Tale. By JANE TAYLOR.
Tuppy ; or, The Autobiography of a Donkey.
Uncle Jack the Fault-Killer.

FOURTH SERIES.—40 Cents each.

Angus Tarlton. A. L. O. E.
Loss of the Australia.
Glory, Glory, Glory.
Child's Book of Divinity.
Collier's Tale.
Cottage by the Stream.
Day-Break in Britain.
Decision. GRACE KENNEDY.
Jessy Allan.   "
Little Walter of Wyalusing.
My Mother's Chair.
Old Gingerbread.
The Pastor's Family.
Helen of the Glen.
The Persecuted Family.
Ralph Gemmell.
The Toll Gate.
Trust in God.
Truth Is Always Best.
The Story of a Needle.
The Two Paths.
True Heroism. By A. L. O. E.
Unica.
Village Home.
Walter Binning.
Wee Davie. By MACLEOD.
Wings and Stings.